MY RIDE.
MY RULES.

The Sky We Look At Is The Same

COURTNEY K. HURST

Dedication

For my Special Ks – my two true loves – Kieran and Keelson

Table of Contents

SUNDAY

Prologue

Dear Reader,

If you had told me in the spring of 2014 that I'd graduate from Carter Prep, run from Rob's house clutching my underwear in one hand while fumbling with my car keys in the other, and then head to college in Boston and not come home for a full year, then I would've said you were crazy.

Back then, I couldn't have fathomed staying away from Wellbury for <u>that</u> long.

Away from Dad. And Gloria. And Ruth.

Back then, I didn't know that change is the only constant thing in our lives. Nor did I know how exhausting it was to figure out who I was, amidst the chaos of change.

I didn't know that juggling different versions of me, and hiding parts of who I had become, would only hurt me.

Now that I know all that, I need to come clean. No more secrets. No more lies.

You need to know my whole, true story if we're going to develop a relationship from here. And once you do, you'll know what I wish I knew sooner: Life is a series of roller coasters, so you better be the one designing the tracks.

FRIDAY

Chapter One

With each mile I drove to my childhood hometown of Wellbury, Conn., from the best summer of my life in the seaside town of Provincetown, Mass., the sun started to sink a little lower in the afternoon sky and the hole in my heart grew a little wider.

In sixty minutes, I'd be back.

Home Sweet Home.

At least it used to be, until thirteen months ago.

Until Dad's annual company barbeque.

Until Rob.

I hadn't been back since it happened, and I had secrets I was terrified of sharing. Staying away from home made it easier to bury them. To try to forget.

I figured out how to hide that I'd changed by avoiding <u>any</u> meaningful connection, even at a distance. By engaging as little as possible with Dad, Gloria, and Ruth, it was easier to pretend that I was still the same person I was before the barbeque. Before I started questioning my every move. Before I started keeping secrets. Before I started waking at night, terrified and anxious, tossing and turning. Before I started partying to outrun the pain.

Before, when the worst trauma I could imagine was facing the heartbreak of someone leaving me.

Before, when I'd look forward to the annual barbeque and its celebration of everything Dad's company had accomplished that year. A celebration of friends and the community in which we, Dad and I, called home. Our small town of Wellbury.

The barbeque. It was the <u>only</u> reason I headed home that week. If I could've, I would've just headed to Boston directly from Provincetown. There was a comfort knowing that my dorm room would be exactly how I left it in May, with only the Polaroids I took from freshman year on the walls. I never hung the photos I brought from home when I moved in. I didn't even take them out of their moving box. I had no roommate, so there was no pressure to decorate.

The first time Alex, the campus "It Girl" who was forced to be my class partner came to my room, she said it was "depressing, like a serial killer lived there." Then, the next day, she showed up with an old-school Polaroid camera for me. I started snapping photos and decorating my walls. Being with Alex made creativity cool and I even thought of writing short stories that started with the objects I photographed - the beer mug on the table, or the book on a blanket in the grass - and then work outward to the people around them, instead of the other way around. The camera gave me a way back into myself that felt safe and private.

I needed to get back to James B. University and the comforts and chaos of campus. I wanted minimal time with my own thoughts in Wellbury. I didn't need reminders of Rob and my last week there. But kicking off sophomore year would have to wait because Dad <u>insisted</u> that I come back for a visit <u>and</u> that it be for this barbeque. After accepting my every possible reason to avoid coming home, he wasn't taking "no" for an answer on this one. Since I loved him, and since he was still footing my bills, I had no reason to not show up for him.

It was only two nights. I'd be gone by Sunday afternoon.

And Rob wouldn't be there.

He hadn't worked for Dad since shortly after I left for Boston. It was the <u>one</u> thing that gave me any peace in my first few months away at college. His unexpected, sudden departure gave me a tiny ledge of consolation to lean on, especially in that first, lonely month. Rob ruined my hometown for me and I didn't want him living there happily while I lived away miserably. It would've made me sick if he was still cruising around Wellbury, working with Dad and hanging at our house, like he had started to do towards the end of my senior year.

He wheedled his way into Dad's life – and by extension mine – because he told anyone who'd listen that he "worshiped" Dad. He'd go on and on about how Dad was his role model, all the while brimming with his own confidence and cocksureness. If only I had seen his self-assured charisma as a flashing warning light instead of a blinking beacon. Until the night of the barbeque, his tight crew cut and chiseled face were hot in a disciplined, orderly way. After the barbeque, all I could see in those features were power and horror.

The "if onlys" killed me. If only Ruth had been at the barbeque as she had been every other year. If only I hadn't started sneaking drinks. If only...I could go all day with these thoughts. Sometimes I did.

At least Rob was gone.

Yet, even knowing he <u>wasn't</u> there, I still wanted to drive slower and slower as I got closer and closer.

As the miles fell behind me, I <u>tried</u> to get excited about seeing Ruth for the first time in a year. When we were young, we'd rarely go more than twelve hours without seeing each other, let alone twelve months. Our entire day revolved around each other from the moment we woke and walkie-talkied "Good morning" to each other; to meeting up in front of our houses to walk to school; to going to every class together and sitting next to each other, if we could; to eating lunch together with a revolving group of acquaintances; to heading home to Ruth's after school to zip through our homework so we could watch old-school movies that we were obsessed with.

Gloria, Dad's best friend, got us hooked on them when she first arrived to help me and Dad put our lives back together after Mom left. I first loved and then loathed Gloria as the years went on. By the time I was a teenager, I would've <u>never</u> given her the satisfaction of knowing we were still obsessed with *Flashdance* and *Beaches,* and all her other old school favorites, so we watched them at Ruth's. We couldn't get enough of them. And we couldn't get enough of each other. Ruth was the sister I never had. She was pretty and confident in her own, nerdy way. Her long, brown hair always pulled back in a fishtail braid; her clothes were always clean, ironed, and tucked. She always had it together. It's probably what kept me from cracking. And I think we both knew it, even if we never acknowledged it.

I think we both always kind of knew that I wasn't like her; that I was always just a step away from stumbling.

I missed those early days and our closeness since we left Wellbury for college. Ruth was family. That hadn't changed. It's just...everything else had. And she had no idea. I was keeping so much from her. From everyone, really, but with her it felt the most severe because we'd always told each other everything.

Well, actually, that's not true.

I'd been keeping secrets from Ruth since high school. It's just that they were smaller things, like saying I loved staying in on the weekends to watch more of the aforementioned movies instead of going to parties and drinking keg beer. Or that I loved studying on Sunday mornings to get a jump on the week. You know, low-stakes stuff that might not have been racy and fun, or even riveting, but kept me by Ruth's side, no matter what she wanted to do.

My recent secrets were far from low-stakes.

As I drove, I wished I had time to stop at Blue Sky, the jetty I used to visit to center myself, but I knew Dad and Gloria had been waiting all day – all year, really – so I skipped it, even if it was just what I needed. As I drove by Exit 3 for Blue Sky, I thought of my first babysitter, Alice, who was Mom's friend from Sacred Art, the art store where she worked. Alice watched me once in a while, which I loved because I adored her. I think she was younger than Mom. Or maybe she just seemed it because she seemed cooler with no kids, an awesome T-shirt collection, and "Happy Hours" at her place every week, which Mom brought me to once in a while, as long as I didn't tell Dad.

Mom said he wouldn't understand and I agreed. He would shake his head at all the dancing and laughing and wildness of those few hours.

I wondered if Alice still had drinks with friends on Friday afternoons and who the new girl in her life was. That made me miss Mom, or at least the version of her that existed in those early (and only) memories of her. Back then, life felt magical. Like anything was possible. That first trip to the jetty with Alice was no exception.

I must've been about five-years old and she was watching me for a whole day <u>and</u> night so Mom and Dad could celebrate their ten-year wedding anniversary. I didn't really care <u>why</u> they needed an overnight together; I was just happy to be with Alice. I didn't want to ever leave her apartment that was so different from the granite and stainless steel at our house. Everything about her place screamed "adventure," just like her. There were trinkets and rugs, furniture and art and dishes from every corner of the world. In the place of photos of kids or pets, there were photos of her laughing and smiling in far-flung places with people of all colors and cultures. Every corner and shelf felt like it held a story. I could've spent hours, imagining where each thing came from.

The day Alice introduced me to Blue Sky, she sold me on leaving her place with fantastic tales of unicorns, mermaids, and fairies in a secret world that existed beneath the jetty that humans couldn't visit or even see, unless they knew the secret password, which she did. That was all I needed to hear and we jumped in her beat up, yellow convertible VW Bug and took off.

When we got off the highway, we drove past every last house and business, until we came to a dead-end where we took a sharp left onto a road that you have to know is there. We drove under a covered bridge, which was a first for me and delighted me to no end. From there, we wound our way towards the jetty and, as we did, the trees got greener, the sky bluer. It felt as if the place itself was alive, bright, and vibrant. It felt like magic.

The road dumped us into a sandy, unofficial parking lot with no clearly marked path, though Alice explained there were many options, once you knew what to look for. That day, I had no idea how much time I'd spend as a teenager, finding and winding my way down those paths, with each one leading to a different stretch of remote beach. All I could think about that first day was how excited I was to show Mom this fantastical spot and I made Alice <u>promise</u> she wouldn't take her there so I could be the one to do it as soon as I could drive. That was the plan my five-year-old self hatched. But life has a way of changing even the best laid plans. Mom left long before I could drive.

Mom's departure was the end of Alice in my life. For a few years after Mom left, I'd see her from a distance, but

I was always with Dad, and we never stopped to catch up. He always thought Alice encouraged Mom to become more active with her arts than her family. I didn't think so. I loved their crazy, fun friendship. Mom was always laughing when she was with Alice. So was I.

I never understood why Dad didn't <u>want</u> to talk to Alice. I understood that he didn't like how much time me and Mom spent with Alice, but I always wondered, *Maybe Alice knows where Mom is*, and, like, why wouldn't he want to ask her? But he never waved or smiled, let alone stopped to talk to her, so I just followed suit.

A decade later I'd get my license and I'd finally go back to the jetty, thinking I might see Alice there, but I never did.

That first day I drove there, I felt so mature. So free. I blasted Rihanna with the windows down, even though it was freezing. I was finally driving solo and doing it exactly how I wanted. I got a glimpse of the years ahead of me and I felt excited and nostalgic at once; old yet young simultaneously.

When I got to the parking lot, that sense of contentment and longing carried me out of the car and onto the beach, where I sat for an hour, despite the chill, feeling brave and mature for adventuring there. It became the place I went for solitude.

I never showed it to Dad, or Ruth, or anyone, until I brought Brendan for our one-month anniversary. But that's not surprising since most "Firsts" were with him. First real boyfriend. First time I had sex. First love. First vacation with a significant other, even if it was with Dad and Gloria and we had separate rooms. First funeral when his aunt died. First wedding when his uncle got remarried. My major Firsts.

Once I showed him Blue Sky, it became our spot. We spent hours on that beach, in all seasons. We even had sex at midnight one summer night, beneath the stars. It was one of the raciest things we did because we weren't supposed to be there at all. Nobody was from 9 p.m. to 6 a.m.

We parked on the side of a road, long before the parking lot, and hiked in with a blanket and a couple beers he stole from his house. We felt like outlaws all the way around, which only added to the sexiness of the night. We were totally in-sync, in a way we hadn't been before. Making love to Brendan always made me feel connected to him in such a special, soulful way, once we got the hang of it; but there was something about that night on the beach. It's like our naked bodies bound together as one between those beach blankets. It was Us against The World and I felt whole, like I was part of something bigger than just me. That was the first night we said we loved each other.

When he left me for Abby, I went to Blue Sky every day for weeks, hoping he'd come to tell me he'd made a mistake. Day after day, I'd sit on the beach crying and waiting. He never came. Of course he didn't. He moved on. He left me, just like Mom did. I should have known. I'm always the one left behind. The one people move on from. The one people forget about.

I took Exit 5 and a deep breath as I rolled around the rotary and onto Main Street, Wellbury. Three miles left. As much as I wanted to resist the place, its rolling green lawns, white picket fences, and blue-shuttered houses pulled at my heartstrings. Home. I rolled down the window so I could smell the salty air, so different than Provincetown's briny breeze. Here, it was infused with the scent of the cedar trees and roses that marked Wellbury's pristine town square, versus the bait and diesel that marked Provincetown's fishing wharf.

It looked like nothing had changed as I passed the Fortune Palace Chinese restaurant that doubled as a bowling alley where everyone had at least two birthday parties from the ages of eleven (when it felt mature to be able to finally go there) to fifteen (when it felt mature to be there without parents). By the time sixteen came, it was over. But the place was a rite of passage for Wellbury kids from eleven to sixteen without a doubt. I wondered if it still was as I approached even more familiar ground.

Coming into our neighborhood, I felt the same butterflies that fluttered in my stomach when I was four-years old and coming to the house for the first time. Now, the nerves were for other reasons. And all those years ago, even though I was nervous, I was mostly excited as we drove into the cul-de-sac, which I had heard Mom and Dad talk about enough to know that it was full of "really good people." Little did I know at the time, Ruth would be one of them.

And little did I know how much I'd love our new house. I didn't even know we needed a new house. I thought the apartment we had in Brooklyn was great because we all slept in the same room with Mom and Dad sleeping above me in a loft. It was like a treehouse. I was sad to leave it, but Mom and Dad hyped up the Wellbury place so much that I was excited to live somewhere new.

Before I even saw our new house, I loved it because I <u>felt</u> the love and excitement between Mom and Dad. It was contagious and a warm feeling started to heat up my chest until it was full-on hot excitement when I walked into my new room. Mom had spent the previous weekend painting it to look like a jungle with all the animals I loved, even if they didn't really live in the jungle.

There were fish having tea parties with owls on palm fronds. Sloths lazing by a river where puppies and butter-flies frolicked, and pandas and koalas playing in the rainfor-est, hiding behind massive and magnificent flowers that didn't exist anywhere except Mom's mind and on those walls. I absolutely LOVED it. Sometimes, I wished I hadn't painted over it. Not that I wanted the daily reminder of Mom, but because it was <u>that</u> cool. And because the rest of the house felt so fancy with its stainless-steel appliances, shiny surfaces and leather furniture. My room felt different. It felt like Mom's studio. Comfortable. Warm.

But not all things are meant to last, I guess.

I still loved my room when the walls were wallpapered with a simpler, saturated yellow. It felt like it was outdoors with its many windows and skylights casting light around the room like an ever-changing kaleidoscope. It had a reading nook where I'd spend hours coloring and, later, studying with Ruth. And then Brendan and I would spend hours there, cuddled up as we broke down barriers and I let him go further and further until we were hurtling towards home base and, therefore, my bed.

That house held it all. It was haunted, but not with ghosts. With memories. Happy, sad, angry, and otherwise. It brimmed with emotion like a living thing, so it always moved me.

Pulling into the driveway that day was no different, just like Dad standing at our door, waiting for me, as he had hundreds of times, whether I was coming home from a sleepover or a trip to the store. I still don't know how he managed to be there, even when he had no clear sense of when I'd be home. "Dad Power." At least that's what he always said.

As I pulled in, my heart warmed at the sight of him. He's the only person I've ever met who has "bright" brown eyes. And his solid summer tan and beaming smile hadn't changed, even if his usually dark hair looked more salt than pepper now. I missed him. It almost felt good to be back. Until I zeroed in on his face.

I knew that look.

Something wasn't right.

As I got out of the car, he walked towards me with his arms out for a hug.

I noticed the cream envelope in his hand but was more concerned with the troubled look on his face.

"Hi, Honey. How was your drive?" he asked as he hugged me.

"It was good. But...are you OK?"

He didn't respond. He was silent. Nothing. He wouldn't catch my eye. This wasn't like him. Even in the toughest times, Dad always had a response. An answer.

I asked again, "Are you OK?"

He handed me the cream envelope. "Brendan and Abby are getting married. He invited me."

Chapter Two

It's fascinating how a place continues on, even when you're not there. Houses change, people disappoint, and old lovers get married.

How was I old enough that an ex was engaged? Why did it feel like a chapter of my life was over in a way it hadn't until then? Would the thought of it always hurt?

As Dad hauled my bags upstairs, Gloria buzzed around the kitchen in her signature look: all-black ensemble with very little makeup except mascara, some blush, and lip gloss. She must've always known that her fiery red, wavy hair against her ivory skin was enough of a visual.

I noticed a new cappuccino machine on the counter. Last I knew, Dad didn't drink coffee. Did he start? Was it for Gloria?

"Can I get you anything?"

"I'll get it if I want it." When I realized I sounded like an asshole, I quickly added, "But thanks."

Gloria didn't seem to notice because she just kept talking. "Didn't you just love PTown? I was there in the eighties and LOVED it, from what I remember, if you know what I mean."

I tried to act like she hadn't already said that at least ten other times since I first said I was going to Provincetown for the summer.

"Yeah, it was great. And it was clutch to be with Alex and her friends, who really know how the locals do it. All the touristy stuff gets old fast when you're trying to work. The extra-long lines everywhere you go. The crowded beaches. The seasick whale watchers coming off the boat and only ordering lemon water. That's all <u>super</u> annoying when you're trying to make money by slinging fish & chips to the masses. It was great to know where to escape to on days off."

"Of course Alex knows. From that FaceTime with her that one time, I understood why you've been so busy. She has an energy about her, doesn't she? I can tell she's all go, go, GO. And...she's absolutely gorgeous. That night I met her on video, I told your dad that she's proof that God does love some of us a little more than others."

"She's actually had a pretty hard life. It's kind of what I appreciate about her. She doesn't give a shit what has happened in the past, she just keeps moving forward. She doesn't look back."

Before Gloria could respond, Dad resurfaced and joined us around the kitchen island. "So, Honey, how was the summer? We want to hear all about it," he asked, not knowing I had just shut Gloria down on that discussion. And what was he talking about, acting like I hadn't spoken to him all summer?

"I texted you guys all the time this summer, and we talked, like, every couple of weeks."

The black-and-white granite of the island shone well enough that I could see our reflections in it. I saw Dad and Gloria smiling. I saw me grimacing.

I tried to smile.

"I know, Honey. I didn't mean to attack you or anything. I'm just chatting."

Gloria jumped in. "I'm glad you're back. But it seems like a summer by the sea suited you."

"I worked a lot. It wasn't endless days at the beach or anything," I spat out before I could refrain. I saw Gloria's smile falter in the granite, so I said, "But, yeah, it was fun."

Gloria shook off my rudeness and kept the conversation going. "I hope you're OK with the changes I made to the barbecue this year. I figured it was time for some changes," she said, and I swear she looked at me, down at the table, and then back at me, in a knowing way, before adding, "You know, with it being the fifteenth anniversary and all."

"I'm sure it will be great, Gloria." I did my best to seem interested, versus sick, at the mention of the barbeque.

"Is everything alright, Elizabeth?" Gloria tilted her head like she did when she thought she had something important to say, which was often.

I mean, where did she want me to start? But instead of admitting <u>that</u>, I said, "I'm just tired."

"You must be. There's a lot going on," she said and looked at the cream envelope that Dad had put on the kitchen table, out of our direct sight. She saw me looking at it and reached for my hand, but I pulled it away and hoped she didn't notice it was to avoid her. I failed. She noticed.

"Well, if you want to talk about anything, let us know." As her voice trailed off, I felt guilty for being a brat to her, as I usually did, after I usually was. I could tell I hurt her feelings, and I hated that. She was trying, like she had been since she arrived a few months after Mom left. And just in time, really, though I hadn't ever admitted it to her, or even to myself.

Back then, me and Dad were struggling. He was exhausted from building his landscaping business, and scared shitless about raising his six-year-old daughter alone. For all the ranting and raving he did to Mom about her lack of schedule with me, he was having trouble creating one.

He was absorbing my fear and the pain of knowing that I couldn't truly count on anyone now that Mom had vanished.

He was operating without a plan, and drinking more than usual. Two beers after work turned into bourbons by the fire until 1 a.m. Alone. The TV illuminating his worn face. He didn't think I saw him, but I did. I saw his empty stare. He had lost himself. A limb had been severed and now he had only me, a little girl whom he struggled to understand. A girl like no one else except the woman who left.

Somehow, we soldiered on.

Kind of.

And then, Gloria came for a long weekend and changed everything. She had wanted to come when Mom first left, but Dad kept telling her that he was fine – we were fine – and a visit would be a kind but unnecessary gesture. At first, she gave him space. But after a while she wouldn't take "not yet" for an answer again and came.

They basically drank and laughed for two days. And Gloria got him outside for long walks on trails we had never explored. It was fun. They talked nonstop the entire time. I don't remember exactly what they were carrying on about, but I remember thinking that Dad seemed OK for the first time in a long time. The fog of sadness that had shrouded our house and hearts since Mom left was slowly starting to evaporate.

Gloria wasn't around when Mom was still home. It's not that they didn't get along or anything like that, but Gloria ran a life coaching business in California and never visited back then. She just never really knew Mom.

Gloria was the college girlfriend of Dad's best friend, Will, so the three of them spent a lot of time together "back in the day." Will and Gloria broke up around graduation, but stayed close enough that Will invited her to his wedding. At that wedding, Dad, Mom, and Gloria hung out and had a blast, or so the story goes. After that, Dad and Gloria rekindled their friendship. They talked often and helped each other grow their new businesses. They were resources for each other and she was very much in Dad's life; just not in mine and Mom's.

On that final night when she came to visit that weekend, I remember feeling sad that she was leaving and when I told Dad he said, "Me too, Honey." We agreed it had been the best weekend we'd had in a long time. It felt like she belonged with us.

The next thing I knew, Dad said, "Well, you could always come back and give the East Coast a try for a while."

I remember the exact words. And I remember Gloria's face as she looked from him to me and back again. "I'm in," she said. Those two words changed my life. They changed all our lives. I just didn't realize the depth of this change until much later.

Apparently, she was looking to expand her business on the east coast, so Dad's invitation was perfectly timed. She didn't know what she was looking for, but there we were. The rest was our (new) family history.

Fast forward fifteen years and there we were still, huddled around the kitchen island. Except, I was holding back more than I ever had. I feared that if I started talking about Brendan's wedding invite, I might kick off a crying jag that I had <u>mostly</u> avoided since I drove out of Wellbury a year earlier. I couldn't admit that the invitation kicked me in the gut. That my heart felt like Brendan's fiancé, Abby, was dancing on it in those stupid black and pink cowboy boots that she wore <u>everywhere</u>. Literally, <u>every</u> time I saw her, she had those stupid boots on.

That was the first clue that Brendan and I were growing apart. We always made fun of country music until one day, after Brendan had started a new job where he loved his "new work crew," there was country music blaring from his radio when he turned his car on. I couldn't even tell you who it was, but it sounded like one of those old, country voices that everyone who loves country loves.

"Gross!" was my first reaction and then, when I realized it was coming from a playlist of his, I asked, "What? This isn't yours, is it?"

"Not all of it is bad," he said in a way that told me he was feeling guilty about more than his changing music preferences.

"We hate country music," I said to remind him, and to hold onto the ways we were a "We."

"Well, I'm starting to like some of it," he said as he scrambled to find another playlist.

We drove away in silence. I was sour. I wished I could be the "Cool Girl" and just let it roll off my shoulders. I wanted to open myself up and say, "Alright, let's give this music a try, if you like it." But I couldn't muster those reactions because, whether he realized it or not, he had mentioned Abby more than anyone in this "new work crew" and it wasn't lost on me that I hadn't met her yet. *Abby is so funny...Abby came from Georgia and rides horses...Abby, Abby, Abby!*

I was pissy all morning and, when he tried to talk to me about it, I acted like everything was OK, but still acted pissy. He eventually got annoyed and said, "Why don't I just drop you off?"

"Why, so you can go listen to country music with your new friends?"

That pissed him off even more, so he drove to my house, pulled up, and said, "Let's just call it a day. There's no sense in spending time if we're just miserable together."

"I'm not miserable," I pouted before realizing just how angry he was. I changed my tact and tried (and failed) to make my pouting cute, which had come off as sexy in the past. He wasn't buying it this time.

"Listen, Elizabeth – I just don't want to hang out anymore today. I'm tired of you getting mad at me because I like my new job," he complained, which he never did.

"I know. I'm sorry. Let's just shake it off."

"I don't want to be an asshole, Elizabeth, but I want to call it a day."

I refused to get out of the car. I knew I should have, for so many reasons, my dignity being the biggest one, but I couldn't will myself to get out.

"Elizabeth, let's just end this day. We've been going at it for hours. You're now pissed at me, but won't say why. What's the point?"

His green eyes were as dark as I had ever seen them as he glared at me.

That finally drove me from the car. I went upstairs and cried, because, even though it was just a silly fight, I knew it was more than that.

That was the beginning of the end for us. The end of nights cuddled in each other's arms listening to Mumford & Sons, talking about all the ways we'd be different, and all the things we'd do together and apart. Endless conversations about our future. Now, he was marrying a girl who wears pink cowboy boots. How did it all go awry so quickly?

It shouldn't have been hard to wrap my head around the fact that he chose her. It was official. She would be Abby Lewis and would ride off into the sunset with him and those stupid boots. I would never be Elizabeth Lewis, no matter how many times I practiced that signature in high school and, though I wouldn't admit it to a single soul, still did once in a while. Not often. But, once in a while, my hand still went there, along with my heart.

I stared at the black-and-white granite of the island and realized I couldn't stand there, pretending to listen to Dad and Gloria any longer. A plan started forming in my head.

"Excuse me, I'm running to the bathroom."

As I hung out, waiting for enough time to pass so it seemed like I was actually going to the bathroom, I noticed Dad's new towels, shower curtain, and rugs, and realized Gloria must've picked them out. They were so her in all their cream and beige glory. She kept her clothes black and her furnishings neutral, that's for sure.

After a few minutes I flushed, washed my hands, and headed back out.

"Ugh, I just got my period. I have to run to the store."

"Oh wait, let me check my purse," said Gloria.

"Thanks, but I'll need a box for the next few days anyway. I'll run out really quick and then be back for the night."

Before they could throw more solutions my way, I grabbed my keys and a seltzer from the fridge, and walked out. I didn't know where I was headed.

But I did.

It was late afternoon on a Friday so they'd all be at work still. I just wanted to drive by. Just to see it. To feel the connection. Maybe that's what I needed to get the engagement out of my head and focus on Dad and Gloria, and then Ruth and her parents, when they all came later that night for dinner.

At the end of our street, I took a left and started the 3.3 miles to Brendan's, as I've done on foot, bike, and car so many times that I can't hazard a guess at how many. We used to jog the route together on Sunday mornings. He made me a jogger. Well, before that, a fight with Dad and Gloria made me a one-time jogger. It wasn't the first fight, but it was the first one that really mattered.

It was the week before sophomore year and I was doing a study course for the PSATs. Since nobody wanted to be at school during summer, including the teachers, we did as much socializing as studying. One afternoon, my study pod started talking about topics for college essays. I was surprised to hear anyone other than Ruth had thought about it already and started to panic that I didn't have anything to write about.

"I wouldn't worry if I were you, Elizabeth," Tina said. "Out of any of us, you have the best essay material. We're all so boring. At least you have a story."

She drove me nuts, always passive-aggressively competing with me and Ruth for top academic honors. And I knew it drove _her_ nuts that she couldn't surpass us, no matter how many hours she put in.

"What do you mean, 'a story'?"

"You know, something juicy for your essay."

"I still don't know what you mean."

"Your mom leaving." As usual, her expressionless face was hard to read.

I sat there, still puzzled.

"Like...you were abandoned, and you still ended up OK. Like, even better than OK, actually. You and your dad are, like, the most awesome daddy/daughter duo with a heartwarming story about banding together to get through your mom leaving. He never got a girlfriend. His sole motivation is you. I mean, it's a great story. Open it up with statistics on how it's usually fathers who leave versus mothers, and then launch into your story. It's college essay gold."

"Thanks...I guess...?" It felt like I was a snow globe that she just turned upside down and now there were emotions and questions flying around my head like snow in a stupid globe.

"Oh, Elizabeth, you look upset. I'm sorry. I thought it would make you feel better that all you have to do is write about your mother leaving, and then share how, despite the trauma, you ended up being the little do-gooder, straight A student that you are."

"Like I said...thanks...?"

Tina kept going. "Like, why <u>did</u> she leave anyway?"

Ruth jumped in. "What does it matter?"

"It doesn't. I'm just wondering. I asked my folks the other night and they said her mom just took off, pretty much. Didn't give much of a reason. I told them that's crazy. Of course there was a reason. But I realized I didn't know it. I figured I'd ask."

Nobody said anything.

"So what's the story?" Tina pressed, looking from me to Ruth and back again.

When it was clear she wouldn't read the room and just drop it, I said, "I don't know."

"Wait. What? Like, really? You don't know? Or, like, you just don't want to talk about it?"

"Tina, why are you being such a bitch?" Ruth came to my defense just as the librarian reminded us that we were supposed to be studying silently. Ruth <u>never</u> swore, but I was glad she did. The topic was mercifully dropped.

But that didn't mean I stopped thinking about it.

By the time I walked into the kitchen a couple hours later, I was fired up to ask Dad. I had never really asked him. I mean, of course I remember the morning he told me she was gone and wasn't coming back. I think. To be honest, I can't remember which parts are real and which parts I've added or deleted through the years because, well, Dad told me one morning, and I cried and cried and cried...and I guess I asked a few questions. Things like, "What do you mean she's gone?" And, "Where did she go?" And other standard questions a six-year-old would ask.

Except I didn't ask the ones I really wanted to ask: "Didn't she love me anymore?" And, "Who would be my best friend now?"

Dad explained that Mom had a lot going on, and needed some space to deal with it all, and that, to be completely honest, he didn't know if she'd ever come back. But he knew she loved me. And I had him. And it all would be for the best.

And...yeah, that was that. We never really talked about <u>why</u> she left again. I could tell Dad was way more upset than he wanted me to know because I heard him crying in the shower. A lot. And I knew we weren't supposed to be eating cereal and takeout for every meal. Sure, it was fun at first, but I knew it wasn't supposed to go on and on. And I did my best to make him happy, like not pushing him to talk about Mom, even if his "She needed space and might not come back," comment was super confusing. But he seemed so matter-of-fact about it all, that I just let it roll for all those years.

But the study pod got me wondering. I realized I had more questions than I realized. Or, really, just the one: Why did she leave?

So that's what I figured I'd lead with. There was no sense in dancing around it. I walked into the kitchen to find Gloria making rice and Dad slicing tuna for sushi rolls. Mom never made meals like this. It angered me even more that she was no longer the one whipping up her own adventurous-if-not-always-delicious-or-even-edible meals in this kitchen – <u>her</u> kitchen – and I didn't even know the reasons.

I stepped in between them and looked directly at Dad. "Why did Mom leave?"

"Well, 'Hello' to you, too," Dad laughed nervously.

"I just realized today that I don't really know why Mom left. I know you said she had her reasons, but...what were those reasons?"

"It's complicated, Honey. She loved you very much."

"Yeah, you always say that. But, like, what's complicated?"

"It's just…I don't know, Honey. I don't know how to start answering that right now…"

"What do you mean, Dad?" I turned to Gloria, "Do <u>you</u> know why she left?"

"Elizabeth, where is this coming from?" Dad asked before she could answer.

"Well, Dad, when the kids at study group tell me that I have a juicy story for my college essay because my mom abandoned me, and they start grilling me on why she left, and I have to admit that I don't know, then it makes me feel like I don't even know my own story. That seems strange to me, now that I'm older. It's my story. I want to know it."

"OK, Honey. Calm down." His eyes dimmed.

"I just want to know what happened."

"There's not much to know, Elizabeth. I wish you wouldn't upset yourself."

"But what is 'Not much to know?' That means there's <u>something</u> to know."

"Honey, I have <u>always</u> put you first, protected you as best I could."

"Again, I turned to Gloria. "What do you know?"

"This is between you and your Dad."

"Whatever, Gloria. You always say that, but since you're always here, you'd think you'd share an opinion once in a while. You love to <u>act</u> like you're my mother but you never actually <u>say</u> anything helpful."

Without a thought beyond, *I need to get away from these two*, I went up to my room, put on the closest thing I had to running shoes, grabbed my iPod to blast my "Pump Up for Studying" playlist, went back downstairs, headed out the front door, and started jogging.

I remember it clear-as-the-clearest-day, and not only because of the fight with Dad and Gloria, but also because, up until that moment, I had <u>never</u> considered jogging. Ever. But in that moment, it felt completely natural. I went all the way into the center of town and was about to turn around and go home when a cramp finally got me. I stopped on the town green to catch my breath and stretch, and considered calling Dad for a pickup.

I pulled out my phone when all of a sudden, I felt a THWACK upside my head. Before I had time to react, I heard, "Shit! I'm sorry. Shit. SORRY!"

Running towards me was the most handsome boy I'd ever seen in real life. He was tanned and blond, and his biceps bulged from the tank top he wore. A tank? None of the boys at school wore tank tops. I guess if they had arms like his, then they would've.

My scowl turned into a smile as I focused on the God-like human running my way.

"I'm so, SO sorry," he shouted as he sprinted towards me.

"It's OK. It's not like you meant it," I smiled.

"Of course not," he smiled back, once he saw that I wasn't pissed. "Let me see your face," he said with a concerned look.

"It kind of hurts actually."

Just then, three other tanned, blonde kids ran towards me; two boys and a girl, all younger than him, or so it seemed.

"This is my family. We're new to town and were just playing football while our parents grocery shop." He gestured to his siblings and they all said, "Hi" at different times like friendly gunfire.

"Hi, Everyone."

"So, yeah, we're sorry," the hunky ringleader said. And his siblings repeated, "We're sorry," like more rounds of amicable ammunition.

"I'm Brendan," he said, stepping even closer with his hand out.

"I'm Elizabeth." I took a step forward and shook his hand. It felt electric.

Brendan winced. "I feel bad. I think that might leave a mark."

"It'll be fine. Don't worry about it," I said, but the whole time I wondered how red I was from my first-ever jog, if my face was swollen and, mostly, how I could keep talking to him.

"So...you just moved here?"

"Yup. We just got here. From California." He motioned to an SUV towing a U-Haul.

"Oh, WOW. Like, you <u>just</u> got here," I laughed and they all laughed.

I was about to ask what school they were going to when a woman yelled, "Hey, Lewis Crew – Let's GO!" She was tanned and blonde too so I assumed she was his mother and that the California stereotype existed for a reason.

"I have to go, Elizabeth! But I'm going to feel bad about this. I hope this doesn't sound creepy, but can you let me know you're OK? Or, actually, should we give you a ride home or something?"

"Oh my GOD. NO! I am <u>fine</u>. But thanks."

"Are you sure? My folks won't mind."

"That's so nice of you, but, no. I'm fine. Really."

"OK. But how about I give you my number and you can let me know you're fine, once you get home?"

I was stunned. Was this a pickup line? It couldn't be! Look at him! Or, was he really that worried? Whatever the reason, I didn't hesitate. I pulled out my phone and got ready to save a new contact.

I started typing. "Brendan...?"

"Lewis," he said and gave me his digits.

"Got it. But don't worry. I'm fine."

"But I will worry." He started to jog towards his family and turned around. "So text me."

I had to make sure I was still on the ground because I felt like I was flying.

I tried to look casual as I stretched a little longer, wondering if he was looking at me still. I pulled out my phone and started walking home. "Hey, Dad. Yup, I'm fine. I'm walking home. I'll see you soon. I'm sorry I flipped out. Please tell Gloria, too."

I walked home with a pep in my step. I could barely feel my cheekbone where the football crashed, but I almost wanted the bruise so I could tell the story over and over again of how I met Brendan Lewis.

* * * *

I was so caught up in my own head that I suddenly realized I was white knuckling the steering wheel and almost at the Lewis' house.

This was foolish, I realized too late. It's not like I'd see him, but still. I probably should've just grabbed my running shoes instead of the car keys and made the jaunt more productive, though that would've been a long run to get the tampons I supposedly needed.

If I could've turned around at that point, I would have. This ride was a bad idea. At least he wouldn't be home. Or...FUCK.

No way.

Is that...? FUCK.

There he was, coming out of his house.

It couldn't be!

FUCK.

Yup, it was his truck. And, yup, it was him.

Maybe he wouldn't see me. I looked AWFUL. I was still salty from my swim that morning and not in a sexy, surfer girl kind of way but more like a dirty, summer cottage kind of way from all my sweating as I cleaned and moved out that morning.

I couldn't let him see me like this.

I was convincing myself that he wouldn't see me, when...he saw me.

I should've slowed down, but as I took my foot off the gas to brake, I calculated his distance from me, my speed, and the probability that I could just keep going...that I could just keep driving.

And that's what I did.

I did a drive-by of Brendan's house in my first hour of being back.

So far, it was <u>not</u> so good.

Chapter Three

As I cruised down Main Street, racked with embarrassment, I passed the ice cream parlor where Mom, Dad, and I used to go all the time.

The first time we went, we had just moved to Wellbury and I was fascinated by the old-timey shop, and the buckets and buckets of homemade ice cream in colors and flavors that blew my little mind. Plus, we could walk to it from our house, which boded well for summer days. I was on cloud nine as I skipped along, happily licking my cherry-vanilla ice cream when I tripped, dropped my cone, and started crying. Not because I was hurt, but because I was shocked by the fall, and probably because my ice cream was ruined.

Mom got down to comfort me instantly.

Dad freaked out. He was so angry that he tossed his cone into a street trash can while ranting and raving: "If nothing means anything to anyone in this family. If we buy things only to drop them and waste them, then fine! I'll do it, too. Who cares, right? It's only money. It's only <u>my</u> sweat, <u>my</u> time, <u>my</u> stress..."

Before he could go any further, Mom stopped cold and said in the sternest voice I'd ever heard her use, "ENOUGH, Mike. Enough. For Christ's sake."

I started crying.

Dad snapped out of it, and looked around, realizing he was out of line. Then we all just kept walking home. We never talked about it again. Not even when we went back for ice cream, which was often. But I thought of it every time. I wonder if Dad did, too.

* * * *

I was back in our driveway before I realized I hadn't stopped for the tampons I didn't really need. What a fucking disaster.

Did Brendan see me?

<u>Of course</u> he did.

Though...I hoped...there could've been a <u>tiny</u> chance he didn't.

Or maybe he <u>thought</u> it was me, but when I didn't stop, he figured he was wrong, and then forgot it even happened. <u>Maybe</u>.

Shit.

I was stressing about whether or not I should text him, but every message I thought of sounded nuts. What could I say? "Sorry I'm stalking you"? Or, "Sorry I'm still in love with you"?

<u>Why</u> did I drive over there? Or, better yet, why didn't I just stop and give a cool, "I heard the wonderful news. Congratulations!" That would've been the mature thing to do. The <u>reasonable</u> thing to do. But, nope, I did a slow, stalking-like entrance followed by a fast, getaway car-like exit. What a fucking IDIOT.

I jumped out of my car, hustled into the house and yelled, "Hey, guys, I'm gonna jump in the shower."

I barely heard Dad say, "Sure, take your time, Honey," as I bolted upstairs to avoid them seeing that I didn't have tampons.

At least making a complete dumb-ass of myself in front of Brendan temporarily distracted me from my anxiety about seeing Ruth that night. But the nerves came crashing back as I got ready for dinner. As much as I'd been avoiding her to not seem different because of Rob, I'd also avoided her because of the interrogation I expected about Alex. I was sure Ruth was chomping at the bit to get the full low-down on this new friend who changed me. Because one thing was certain: Even if we'd been mostly emailing and texting since we parted ways, and even if I hadn't told Ruth about the night of the barbeque, or about the ins and outs of my partying with Alex, I could tell that she could tell that <u>something</u> was different, and I knew because of the questions she asked and that I avoided, that she wanted to get to the bottom of it.

Prior to us actually arriving at our separate schools last fall, we always figured that, separate schools or not, we'd still talk <u>every</u> day. But in those first few days, when she arrived on the Vassar College campus and was loving it and busy and social, and I was reeling from Rob and trying to force myself through the motions of packing up and heading to school myself, our daily phone check-ins never happened. We played endless games of phone tag until we realized that emails were best if we had a lot to say and texts were better for quick thoughts. That's how we kept in touch, which was perfect for me. I could cull and curate what I wanted to share.

I got good at it. Not only with Ruth, but with Dad and Gloria, and everyone, really; even myself. But that night with Ruth, I wouldn't be able to narrate my one-sided version of how I was. I'd be face-to-face with her, the person who knew me better than anyone. The person who knew how I *should* act.

Growing up, we were well-liked, but not popular by <u>any</u> mainstream method of measurement. We were welcomed in all groups, but never topped anyone's VIP list.

Or, really, any guest list at all. I always told myself it's because we kept to ourselves and didn't care about all the popularity stuff. At least Ruth didn't, and I mirrored that, on the outside. But on the inside, I always wondered what it would be like to be popular. I daydreamed about Lisa, the captain of the cheerleading squad who always perfectly coordinated her shoes and watchband, walking up to me at lunch and saying, "Come join us."

I bet that most people who graduated with me would be surprised that I spent any time daydreaming about that. But, yeah, secretly, I <u>wanted </u>to be included in the nights when our classmates were having fun and pushing boundaries. I wanted to see what my normally wavy brown hair would look like after a friend took a curling or flattening iron to it. What would my blue eyes look like with more makeup than I knew how to apply? What would Ruth look like if her hair was in something other than a braid? How would her freckles look if she were flush with booze, like the glow from a good time that I'd seen so many classmates roll into dances with? How would she act when she wasn't trying to act perfectly?

A couple times, in middle school, I suggested to Ruth that maybe we should try to get an invite to a party and see what it was like. She said, "No thanks. I don't need to stand around in a cold basement, watching everyone get drunk and make out with people they barely talk to when they're sober. Gross. That sounds like a nightmare."

I was like, "Yeah, you're right. Totally."

I don't know why I never said, "I think it sounds like fun. Why don't we just try it?" I guess I didn't want to do anything that would make her not like me; that would make her leave me. I should've known that, ultimately, she would. I mean, it was just to get a boyfriend and, as her best friend, I should've been happy for her, and I was. But I just didn't understand – and still don't – how she changed our routine so quickly and unexpectedly.

One moment Ruth and I were sitting in the bleachers at a "Freshman Spring Fling" that I forced her to go to even though neither of us planned to dance. The next moment our dorky classmate, Roger, who we had never even really spoken to before, was asking Ruth to dance.

By the time the weekend was over, they had agreed to be boyfriend and girlfriend.

By the end of the week, he joined us after school to study and hang out.

By the following weekend, they saw *Bridesmaids* without me. *Bridesmaids?*! A chick flick about friendship! And she went with Roger. I was crushed.

Ruth ripped the friendship rug out from under me. She tried to include me sometimes, but I was pissy because, like, Roger should've been joining <u>us</u>. *He* should've felt like the third-wheel. Not me! Until Roger, Ruth and I did everything together from the time we woke to the time we slept. Every. Single. Day.

Then, one day: Boom! Roger was in. I was out.

They were inseparable. I was hurt, but stuffed it down. I told myself that Ruth's abandonment didn't feel like the Abandonment I felt when Mom left. That I felt more secure now that I was older. That Ruth was a friend and not a mother. That it's unnatural to leave a daughter for no reason but natural to leave a best friend for a boyfriend. I told myself all those things. But it still sucked. It still hurt. At first.

When I met Brendan, it hurt a lot less. And I understood falling head-over-heels for someone and wanting to spend <u>every</u> free minute with them. For the first time, I understood feeling like a physical extension of someone, and how good that felt. I got it.

And then: BOOM. As sudden as "RuthAndRoger" started, they stopped. Ruth broke up with Roger one day with little warning or fanfare. She said she got bored, and college was coming, so it was time to part ways. It seemed so random and sudden that I pushed her for more of an explanation, but she just said, "It ran its course." With that one simple statement, just as dramatically as she exited my life, she reentered it.

Except, I had another life by then, with Brendan. And I was resentful that Ruth wanted to go back to how it used to be before she disrupted everything about us without any notice or care. But before I got too high-and-mighty with Ruth, Brendan started drifting towards Abby. I saw it coming. The pain of it steered me towards my safe harbor: Ruth and the Millers. We picked up where we left off…

…except…

…things had already shifted.

What used to come so natural – spending tons of time together – was no longer quite the same. It wasn't bad, per se. But it was different. We were different.

* * * *

I was about to do a cold rinse in the shower to shock me into readiness for Ruth's arrival when I heard the doorbell ring and realized I didn't need it; the *DING DONG* sent more than enough adrenaline coursing through my body. I hurried to dry off, ran a comb through my hair, and was giving myself a pep talk about just enjoying the time together after so long apart, and not worrying about how I seemed, or what I was hiding from her, when I heard, "Knock, knock – I hear my friend Elizabeth is <u>FINALLY</u> back in town."

The door joining my bathroom and bedroom was closed, which I was relieved about because, without waiting for a response, Ruth came into my bedroom, like she had for more than a decade. Ruth was even more modest than me so being greeted by my naked body would've horrified us both. Alex was the complete opposite. I pretty much saw her naked every morning <u>and</u> evening this summer as she hurried around the condo, figuring out what to wear while still managing to dance around to the *Aurora* album by Daisy Jones & The Six. She was <u>always</u> running late, and was <u>ob-sessed</u> with that album, so this was a twice-daily event all summer. And don't get her started on her theory that she could "very well be the love child of Daisy and Billy" unless you had time to kill. Sometimes I thought she believed it. And then, there were even times when I did too. Wild.

I put on the sweatpants and hoodie that were in the bathroom already, thankful that I had something to wear besides a towel for the greeting.

"Hey, I'll be right out!"

"Hurry up. You've made me wait long enough this year!"

I fought back tears that were brewing due to nerves, and because her voice booming from my bedroom into the bathroom was such a familiar and comforting sound. I splashed cold water onto my face to kill any potential tears, patted it dry, rolled my shoulders back and smiled at my-self. I thought, *It's showtime* as I opened the door to my bedroom.

"Hey-ooo!" I shouted.

Ruth jumped up, rushed at me and wrapped her arms around me before I had time to flinch or fight back tears. After a few seconds, I realized that, if I didn't pull it together quickly, then I'd unleash a year's worth of sobbing that neither of us were ready for. I wanted to pull away from her, but I was nervous to look her in the eye, which only made me more aware of how upset I was, which only made me shakier.

"Hey, hey...Elizabeth...are you OK?" She pulled away from me and held me at arm's-length, gently gripping my shoulders, which snapped me out of vulnerability.

"I'm fine. I just missed you," I said as nonchalantly as possible.

She wrapped me back into another quick hug. "I missed you too."

We then moved to my bed, shoulder to shoulder against the headboard, and the months fell away.

"Tell me everything," Ruth said. "Start with the summer. We barely spoke, but it sounds like you had the time of your life."

"I did. It was great. But..."

"What?"

"I just did something SO STUPID."

"What?" She side-eyed me.

I put my pillow over my face.

"Tell me!"

"Well, I'm sure you heard that Abby and Brendan are getting married."

"Shit. Yes. My parents told me last week that they heard, but I wasn't sure. And you and I haven't spoken since, and it seemed strange to message, so…"

"It's cool. Don't worry about not telling me," I said, meaning it. Even if she had called last week, I probably would've blown off the call.

"What were we talking about?" she asked. "Oh, that's right, you did something stupid. What did you <u>DO</u>? Is it Brendan-related?"

I put my hands over my face and she demanded again, "What did you do?!"

I kept my hands where they were and said, "I drove by his house."

"You WHAT?! Wait…what? When? Today? Like, on purpose? Oh, Elizabeth, do you still have feelings for him, after all this time?"

"No, I just…"

"I thought you were finally over him. It sounded like you and Alex had put Brendan – and all of us, really – in your rearview mirror."

I ignored the dig and plowed on. "I <u>am</u> over him. I don't know why I drove by. I mean,

I didn't necessarily plan it. I was..."

"You were what? Hoping he'd see you and call off the wedding?"

"Of course not. I didn't even think I'd see him."

"Wait. You saw him?!" She squealed again and then started laughing, which made me laugh.

"Yes."

"What did you say?" she asked incredulously.

"I didn't say anything."

"Wait, what?"

"Ruth, I just drove by. I didn't stop. I slowed down, and then realized how awful I looked and how shady it must've seemed that I was driving so slow, so I sped up and drove away." We started laughing so hard that we were snorting. God, it felt good to laugh with her again.

When we finally stopped, Ruth asked, "Oh my GOD. What will you do? Will you call him? Text him?"

"I don't know. I'm mortified. Honestly."

"Oh, it's not that bad," she said, and then busted out laughing again.

"Yeah, it is," I said through more fits of laughter.

"Yeah, it is," she howled.

When we finally regained composure, she said, "Oh, my friend, I've missed laughing with you."

"I was <u>just</u> thinking that."

"I miss you."

"I miss you, too."

"Where'd you go, Elizabeth?"

"What do you mean?" I stalled as the giddiness wore off and the defensiveness creeped in.

"This year. Where'd you go? You got so distant. I was worried about you. I worried that I did something wrong. I couldn't figure it out. Was it Alex? I know you two are having fun, but is it all under control...?"

"What do you mean? Yeah. Of course."

"OK. Good. Well, how are classes? Like, I don't even know. We barely talk about actual school. My political science classes are kicking my ass. Are yours?"

"They're hell. I hate them."

"Hate them? Whoa."

As breezily as I could, I responded, "Yeah, I really don't enjoy them. I'm slogging through, but I'm not into it at all. I might even change my Major. I'm really into a writing elective I'm taking with a cool professor. You'd love her. Dr. Lisa Rogers. She's a total badass."

"Is Alex in that class?"

"It's actually how we met."

"Is she a 'writer'?" Ruth asked condescendingly, as if the air quotes weren't enough.

"No, she's still Undecided, if you mean her major."

Ruth stopped to think. "That makes sense. That's the impression I get of her."

I wouldn't take the bait. Instead, I tossed my own.

"The class, and meeting Alex, and this summer...it all changed me," I said. As my voice cracked, I added, "A lot has changed for me this year; yet stayed the same somehow. Like writing. It's new but familiar. It's hard to explain. But... I don't know. I kinda don't recognize myself anymore."

"I get it. But, like what? I feel like you want to tell me something."

"Not really. I don't know. I guess, yeah, a lot has changed this..."

"Yup. Got that part. What did you say about changing your Major?"

Ruth was so focused on <u>what</u> I said that she missed the emotion underlying it. I didn't know if I was more relieved or annoyed.

"I don't know. I'm thinking about it."

"Would you still go to law school?"

"No. Well, not right away at least. I don't know." I started to get worked up. How could I tell her that there was so much more to me changing my Major, when I'd kept so much from her so far? How could I explain that last semester, after a particularly torturous night of alternating bouts of flashback nightmares and insomnia, followed by a particularly awful day, I stress-ate an order of mozzarella sticks, a small pizza, and some iced cinnamon sticks, and then made myself throw it all up? It was the first time I did it. But I had pre-planned it. Feeling out of control and stressed out, I wanted to self-destruct and then fix it.

I thought I was alone, but while I was in the bathroom, Alex came into my room using the key I forgot I had given her. She saw the empty food containers on my bed, heard me puking, and added it all up. When I opened the bathroom door, we came face-to-face. I tried to brush her off, but she wasn't having it. She made me sit down to talk about it.

It was a humbling, jarring enough moment that I haven't made myself throw up since. Alex told me that I'm one of the lucky ones since that's all it took. I'm grateful for that. It was her "Closet Theory" that got to me. She explained that we all have an emotional closet, and if we keep opening the door and tossing things in, then slamming the door shut, without ever organizing anything, then eventually, it will all pile and jumble up. Then, one day, when you open the door to throw in one more thing, it will all come crashing down on you because it's so full and disorderly.

That night, Alex asked, "Are you sure law school is best, right after college? Maybe take a break, process some things. You've been soldiering on since your mom left, but maybe it's time to quit soldiering and start sorting through those emotions. You're barely opening the closet door as you toss in another thing."

That night changed everything.

But before I could think about it any further, or Ruth could say anything else about my changing Major, Mrs. Miller yelled up the stairs, "Girls, come hang out with us!"

We both groaned and rolled our eyes. "Be right there," we said in perfect unison, like an old jingle you never forget.

When we got downstairs, everyone was sitting in the living room. Mr. Miller tried to jump up to hug me but I put my hands out and said, "Really, stay sitting," with such force that everyone noticed. But at least neither he nor Mrs. Miller tried to hug me. I just wasn't ready.

"Before I sit down, I'm grabbing a seltzer," I said. "Does anyone need anything?"

I got "nos" all around as I headed to the kitchen. I was on edge. How would I get through the next few hours? All their questions? All of us staring at each other, sharing?

Without giving it too much thought, I grabbed a can of club soda, cracked it open, poured a little down the drain, and quietly reached above the fridge, into the booze cabinet. I grabbed the Ketel One and topped off my can. Then, I took a shot directly from the bottle. Ruth walked in as I lowered it from my lips.

She laughed nervously. "Did you just slug booze from that bottle?"

"No," I laughed too, hoping it would end there.

"You didn't?"

I grabbed my can before she could smell it and calculated my risk. I might as well admit to part of it. "Yeah, I took a quick sip. I had a ROUGH night. I needed a little hair of the dog. Do you want some?" I tried to sound confident and nonchalant.

"Maybe later," she said with a tone that told me "later" would never come.

Before we headed back into the living room, I said, "Please don't tell them."

"Obviously," she said with judgment.

When we got back to the living room, Ruth's dad cleared his throat and in one gesture, pushed his glasses up to the bridge of his nose and then through his pin-straight, brown, bowled hair, like he did when he wanted our attention. Mr. Miller was a quiet man, so when he did want to speak, he got our instant attention. "Cheers. Welcome home you two, and especially Elizabeth. You were missed."

Ruth's stony stare took any potential emotion out of it for me as we all clinked glasses and cans. Obviously, she was still skeptical about the shot she caught me doing.

To quash my anxiety and try to sound normal, I asked, "What's for dinner? I assume pizza since it's Friday?"

"Bingo," Dad answered. "There's a delicious new place we've been ordering from. You'll love it."

"Sounds good. Do you want me to grab it?" I offered. I figured if I kept moving, I'd have to field fewer questions.

"Sure," Dad said.

Ruth jumped up. "I'll come."

We left Dad's and walked out the door.

"Should I drive?" Ruth asked.

"I'll drive," I smiled and got in the car.

"Are you sure you're OK?" she asked once we were in the car.

"Yeah, I'm fine. I had, like, a sip."

Ruth was silent.

"Look, don't overthink that whole thing back there. I was just taking the edge off. I'm exhausted and a little anxious..."

She cut me off. "Yeah, I am too. I don't know how I'll manage sophomore year. Everyone says it's ten times harder than freshman year. How can that even be? I'm excited and terrified."

<u>Of course</u>, she brought it back to herself. And, of course, back to academics. Was she <u>always</u> like this? So singularly focused? Or was it just more obvious to me now?

I turned on some tunes and we pulled out of the driveway, unusually silent. At least, I don't remember us being silent much. Actually, that's not true, we spent so much time together that there were many silent periods, but they were comfortable. Unlike this one.

She turned up the music a little before settling into her seat. She knew all the lyrics to *Rather Be* and I almost asked her if Clean Bandit and Jess Glynne came to her campus as they did ours, but I was enjoying the peace of the moment too much to disturb it.

When we got to the new pizza place, I threw the car in park, left it running, and said, "I'll zip in. Be right back."

It smelled amazing when I walked in the door. The music was pumping and the place was buzzing. The host informed me that takeout orders were at the bar. I cringed because I hadn't changed from the sweats I put on after my shower. Jeez, Gloria could've warned me that I'd have to cross the dining room to grab the food.

I set my gaze on the bar and walked forward without looking left or right to avoid connecting with anyone I might know. It was a great plan, except as I approached the bar, saw the "To Go" sign and headed that way, I zeroed in on the bartender and, yup, it was Brendan.

He worked HERE!?!? What were the fucking chances?

My first thought was, "Run!" If I hadn't already pulled that once earlier, and if our name wasn't on the damn take-out order, then I probably would have. But I couldn't do that twice in a day. Could I?

Before I gave it a third thought, Brendan looked towards me, smiled, and waved. My heart nearly popped out of my chest. It was all I could do to keep my slow, confident pace as I crossed the room. I wanted to run to him. That smile. I had forgotten how that smile could light up a room. I was still a decent distance away when I heard, "Aw, look. Lovebirds reuniting."

What? Wow! I turned to see who was shouting this to us ex-lovers. I didn't realize anybody would even remember when we dated. It was so long ago that...

That's when I saw her.

Abby.

She was coming out of the bathroom, slightly to the left and behind me. I heard those stupid cowboy boots tapping loudly with each step before I saw them.

Brendan was walking towards her and waving. At her. Not me.

It <u>could not</u> happen again. I <u>could not</u> look like a stalker again that day.

In a brilliant stroke of luck, Brendan got pulled back into the kitchen. I was relieved, but my heart raced and my palms sweat as I imagined all the ways it could still go wrong. I was <u>not</u> ready to see him, let alone her. Let alone them together.

I was barely keeping my shit together when I approached the takeout section. There were a bunch of boxes lined up. I hoped one was ours. I said my name as quietly as possible to the server who looked in charge. I'd never loved Dad's anal-retentive ways more than when they said, "You're all set. It's paid and tipped," and handed me the pizzas.

Without looking left or right, I did a tight 180-degree turn, centering my gaze on the door as I walked toward it. I didn't let my eyes budge one bit.

I didn't realize I was holding my breath until I pushed the door open, stepped outside, and sucked in a huge gulp of air. I kept it cool, in case they were watching me leave. I imagined Brendan telling Abby I was stalking him earlier and them laughing at me, or, worse, pitying me.

I opened my car door in one smooth motion and handed the food to Ruth as she said, "Oh my God! Did you just see her?"

"I saw both of them. He works here?! He's the fucking bartender?!"

"Oh, Elizabeth."

I was shaking a little as I pulled out, grateful that Ruth wasn't being her usual "Don't focus on the negative; stay positive" bullshit.

"Did they see you?"

"I don't want to talk about it right now. Let's just get out of here."

I could feel Ruth watching me. If I looked at her, I'd lose all composure. I kept driving. At the red light, she put her hand on my back. I started to sing the ABCs to distract myself from crying.

How would I get through the next two days if they were anything like today? If everything continued to go wrong? And completely unexpected?

* * * *

After Ruth and the Millers left later that night, and I was starting to stress about sitting around and catching up in earnest with Dad and Gloria, Dad got a bunch of business calls, and disappeared into his office while Gloria and I cleaned up and chatted, mostly about the Millers, thank God.

Dad came out of his office in a rush and apologized that he needed to sleep and leave unexpectedly for Boston at dawn. He kissed me good night and headed upstairs. Alone in the kitchen with Gloria, I dramatized my yawn as a sign that I was ready to wrap it up, which she read and respected. As she gathered her things and hugged me good-bye at the door, I wondered, for the first time in a long time, why didn't she just live here? She was always here or they were on the phone, like any pair of best friends. Or were they lovers now? Could they be? Surely, they could be. It wasn't impossible, and of course I had wondered at times, especially when friends would ask why they <u>weren't</u> together. I'd say, "They're just better as best friends." But was that still the case?

As Gloria left, I wondered more than ever if she was lonely. Did she want companionship and just hadn't found someone yet? Did someone hurt her like Mom hurt Dad? Did someone abandon her too?

I closed the front door, surprised I could hear Dad snoring through the floorboards and smiling that some things never changed, like Dad going hard all day and then, as soon as he hit the bed, being dead to the world until that alarm clock went off. He often joked that I could've gotten away with a lot more in high school if I had tried; I just needed to wait until he had fallen asleep.

Then I was exactly where I didn't want to be: home and alone with my thoughts.

I figured I'd sleep my way through it and headed to bed. As I shut the kitchen light off, I saw that, in Dad's hurry, he had left his office light on and his door open. I wandered towards it, wondering just how many times the door was slammed over the years. How were the hinges strong enough to withstand the pushes and pulls of Mom and Dad's passion?

As I flicked the switch to turn off the fluorescent bulb that hung so delicately over Dad's desk, I saw, for the first time in my life, that his safe was wide open.

In so many ways, I wished I had turned around at that moment, walked back upstairs and tucked myself into bed. In so many ways, I wished I could forget what I found. I wished I was back in Provincetown with Alex. I wished I could channel the peace from my swim that morning. But no matter what, I couldn't. I was alone in Wellbury, and Provincetown felt like a fucking lifetime ago.

Chapter Four

When I first moved to Boston for college, I was so lonely. The sky seemed a shade too dark. The classrooms were a bit too claustrophobic, as if the walls were constantly moving closer together. And I didn't really know what was happening <u>inside</u> my body. But I wasn't me. I wasn't right. Something was broken. Unfixable.

The weekends were brutal. I'd be sitting on my bed, alone, and I'd hear girls going from room to room, trying clothes on, getting ready to go out. I didn't know how to jump in. At first, I was happy that my single suite had its own bathroom, especially when I couldn't imagine sharing space with a stranger. But as the weeks went on, I wished I <u>didn't</u> have my own bathroom so there'd be more opportunities to interact with other girls on my floor. Maybe if I were coming out of the shower and someone was putting on makeup, there'd be an opportunity for a "What are you doing tonight? Nothing? You should come with us!" But those kinds of on-the-fly invites never came.

And then Alex and I were forced to be partners and everything changed.

Until then, Alex and I flew at different social altitudes. She soared high and I cruised low. But because we were both absent the same day in Dr. Rogers' "Intro to Writing" course – the day the class partnered up for a semester-long, super personal assignment – we <u>had</u> to partner together. The assignment was to interview your partner about their life and then design an amusement park ride based on a theme, moment, or phase of their life.

Even though I didn't really know Alex, I knew of her. Everybody did. She was hard to miss for a couple reasons. First, she's a stereotypical blonde bombshell from head to toe. She has a face that suits any hair style, which she rotates often, and her gray eyes look lavender against her cream skin; her pouty, perfectly pink lips look runway-ready whether she just rolled out of bed or was dressed to the nines. She has a tiny, tight body with curves. She is gorgeous. Absolutely gorgeous. And once I knew her, I knew that it takes her no time at all to look that good.

She's the kind of girl who can pull off plucking a fresh flower while walking, put it in her hair, and rock it all day, forgetting about it until yet another compliment is given.

Totally unplanned. Raw. Beautiful. And then, because she's always snapping photos, she's got an even cooler vibe. She's <u>in</u> every moment, capturing and making meaning of it. All effortlessly. I never made anything look that easy. She radiated confident and cool vibes like the sun radiated rays of goddamn sunshine.

When she made her entrance on the first day of freshman orientation, she rolled in with friends frolicking around her. Most people were with their roommate and maybe one or two people from their floor. I rolled in alone.

Alex and her crew looked like they had been friends forever, so I assumed she was a sophomore speaker. But the program ended and she never stood up to talk to us. And then I kept seeing her at the other orientation events. She was actually a freshman. She would pop into different groups of people, looking like she'd known them her entire life. Everyone wanted to be around her, which was clear from thirty-feet away.

I was scared to be her partner for such a personal project. How could I truly open up to her? How do you get vulnerable with one of the coolest girls in your class? Alex was cooler than "cool." For weeks I watched from afar and wondered how some girls like her had it all figured out. I'd watch her and ask myself, *How do I get in with that group, now that Ruth isn't here?* I was ready for change. I was ready to do whatever <u>I</u> wanted, just like Alex seemed to do.

When I finally met her that day we were assigned partners, I told her that I always knew who she was. In turn she asked, "Did you just transfer here or something?"

"No, I've been here since the start of the year."

"Wow. OK. But you're new to this class, right? You just transferred into this class?"

"Nope. I've been here since the start of the year."

"Wild. I guess I didn't notice you before. No offense."

"None taken."

"You must be quiet."

"I guess."

"Well, it's nice to meet you <u>now</u>, E."

Nobody had ever called me "E." I hated being called "Liz" and corrected people right away. But "E" – especially from Alex – sounded alright. It dulled her earlier insult, but I was still weary. She must've read it on my face because she said, "I'm sorry. I didn't mean to be rude. I always just say what I think. There is no filter between my mind and my mouth. I'm sorry. I should've said, 'It's nice to meet you. I can't wait to get to know you.'"

I decided to give her another chance.

However, she promptly blew that one, too, when she was impossible to track down to work. I was patient and accommodated her busy (social) schedule, until I wasn't.

Even though, in some ways, my patience running out had nothing to do with her.

I had just talked to Dad who was grumbling that Rob was gone and that he just didn't get it, because it seemed so sudden. It was making his life harder, which was making breathing harder for me, because I didn't know how to reconcile that I was happy Rob was gone, even if it was stressing Dad out. After all, I was hyper-aware of Dad's ongoing joke that, "Luckily, my business started expanding from houses to hotels just in time for Elizabeth to hit the college years."

The wedge between us grew larger, without him even knowing there was a wedge in the first place.

When we hung up, I looked at my watch and realized that Alex was, yet again, late for our meeting. When I called her, she was like, "Oh, SHIT! I completely forgot. Can you try me again tomorrow and we'll see what works?"

I <u>lost</u> it. I called her rude, selfish, and lazy. Then I added entitled and unaware. After I ranted and raved, she was like, "Wow! OK. Don't hold back. Damn, Girl!"

I started to apologize but she was like, "Don't you dare apologize. I didn't know you had that in you. I'm impressed, E. And, you know, you're right. I am all those things. I know it. Nobody really calls me on it. But I get it. Can we start over? I'll meet you there in about fifteen minutes? I'll come right away."

She showed up, and we laughed at my expense about the outburst and then got down to work. Since we were behind, we condensed a lot of work into a little bit of time and got used to sharing our lives with each other. She was an only child, like me. Her father died when she was young, leaving her enough money to live comfortably for life. Even though we were still just scratching the surface, I could see beneath the veil. There was a vulnerability alongside the bravery. There was something courageous, but unsettled, about her. Whereas my first impression was that we had nothing in common, I started to sense that we had a lot in common, even if our main difference was obvious: She wasn't waiting for anyone to tell her who she was; I still needed that outside reassurance.

And she didn't let her past traumatize her.

She never told me a complete, cohesive story about her childhood, but I knew from bits and pieces that there were some very unsafe situations with her mother's boyfriends on the rare weekends she went home from boarding school. Situations where she was forced to act like a woman while she was still a child. She talked about it all like it happened to someone else. It's not that she didn't show emotion, but it was always controlled. Her voice – and her story – were in her control.

One night I asked, "How did you keep going after all that? How can you even talk about it so nonchalantly?"

She didn't hesitate with, "I decided a long time ago that those bastards don't get to keep winning, to keep controlling me. And if I let what they did change me, or make me fearful or ashamed or whatever, then they kept winning. Fuck that. Fuck them."

I started crying. Gut-wrenching, full body sobs. I couldn't stop, even if I wanted to. And I wanted to. I wanted to be as strong and as cool as Alex was.

Without saying a word, she got up, crossed the room, kneeled in front of me so we were eye level, and said, "They don't get to win. You hear me? Whatever happened to you...whatever it was...and you don't have to tell me, but whatever it was, they don't get to win."

I cried even harder and let her hug me tight.

We didn't mention it again. And when we were done with our work, we decided the other's amusement park ride was a carousel, spinning through time with familiar faces never staying long enough to hold. I wonder if we'd write them differently months later, once we knew each other even better. Would I be more, or less, honest? When I wrote hers, I consciously tried to make it seem whimsical instead of sad. I'd probably still do that today. Who wants to make anyone feel sad about their life? Though, I don't think she took the same consideration with my feelings when she wrote mine. Or maybe I was just too sensitive. Either way, we both got As.

Then we started hanging out even when we didn't have any work to do and, before I knew it, we were inseparable. One night, drunk on some fancy birthday champagne that her mom sent in lieu of a promised visit, she told me that I was her best friend. She got all emotional about it, saying she never had any real, true friends until me. It was sweet, even if it made me feel disloyal to Ruth at first, because, well...I never thought it was possible to have more than one best friend. It defeats the purpose of "best" if there's more than one. But then I met Alex and I could see that we get different things from different people at different times. And that meant that more than a few people were "best" for you. It defied grammar. What could I say? I made peace with it.

Between befriending Alex and loving Dr. Rogers' writing class, that semester changed my life. My eyes opened to how much I wanted to experience – and then write about – in this lifetime. And, gratefully, the memories of Rob and Mom faded, not fully, but enough.

Almost overnight, I had a social life. People started saying, "Hey," and chatting me up as I made my way to classes. So much so that I had to build more time into getting to class because I was stopped more often. For weeks,

I was anonymous and then BOOM; I was in a different social set. I was Alex's best friend, which I soon learned was a full-time job. With Alex, <u>every</u> day was about being "all in" on whatever we were in on. It was thrilling. And exhausting. And, sometimes, stressful.

Mid-way through second semester, I sat Alex down at dinner in the cafeteria, on a sober weeknight, and told her that I needed to break our party pace so I could keep my 4.0 GPA (back when that was still an option). I didn't know how to say that I felt like I was spinning out of control, that at first the partying helped distract me, but lately it had been stressing me out; putting me in a bad place. Sure, with my grades. But, with so much more. So much I couldn't figure out for myself, let alone explain to someone else, especially when that person partied without pause to avoid pondering anything. But I figured I'd give it a try.

Alex listened to my case and then leaned across the table towards me, "I hear you. I hear you. And I want you to feel good and be happy. I do. But...and don't think I'm shitting on your lil' speech, but...I have to make the case here that, all of those things made sense for you when you were Pre-Law. Now, you're a Writing Major. What serves you best <u>now</u>?"

She let a beat pass before adding, "If you want to be a writer, you need to LIVE first. You need something to write about. You need more life experience."

I mean, she had a point. But I countered with, "If I'm going to be a writer, then I also have to practice discipline. I have to sit down and actually do the work."

Her reply: "Be a badass, Elizabeth. Make your writing about an epic adventure, like Cheryl Strayed. How are you going to find and forge your own path, and then write about it, if you never leave your room because you're always studying and resting?"

I didn't have the heart to explain to her that hiking the Pacific Crest Trail sober and alone is a far different adventure than the bar crawls Alex had in mind for me. But, of course, the conversation went her way because, ultimately, I didn't want to disappoint Alex. I mean, I rarely rocked the boat with anyone, but especially not with her. That's how I always ended up saying, "OK, let's go!" even when my first reaction was, "Hell no." And then, without fail, I'd end up having so much fun. Every. Damn. Time.

And, of course, it's easier to ignore the pain when you're too busy having fun to dwell on it.

I was always glad that I went out. Alex was a good time. She was the <u>most</u> fun.

When I met Alex, I started to shift from feeling hopeless to hopeful. From lost to found.

And I kept leaning into that. Except, I started leaning so far that I started toppling over.

* * * *

It was hard to believe that I was <u>just</u> swimming with Alex yesterday morning. That I had just heard her signature, "Caw-caw...caw-caw," from the kitchen as I rolled over and tried to ignore it so I could sleep. We had just gone to bed at 3 a.m.

No such luck.

She was at my ear whispering, "Time to swim last night off. It's a big day today," like she had <u>every</u> morning since we arrived in Provincetown, no matter how much I wanted to sleep, or if it was stormy out, or anything at all. And I always got up when she gave the call. At first, I did it for her. But after a while, I did it for me. Those morning swims were good for my soul.

Waking around 8:30 a.m., slightly hungover and ready to swim it off. Throwing on our bathing suits, wrapping towels around our waists, heading out to the beach, and forcing the seagulls to scatter for us before they'd scatter for the onslaught of tourists later. Plunging both feet into the cool, morning-misted sands, and then ripping our towels off and racing full-force to the edge of the water, hesitating for a millisecond before diving in.

I loved being the first one in the water, treading water solo for a few seconds. I'd face the horizon, take a deep breath and center myself as best I could. That time was all mine. Free from the memories holding me down. Free from the nightmares that had haunted me after the barbeque. Free from scrutinizing the changing and different versions of me. Free from the hangover that started the day. Free.

Then, I'd make a long dive to the bay's bottom and grab some sand for good measure, before pushing up and gliding back to the surface to find Alex, treading water and ready to trade memories from the night before.

Committing to the morning swim was one of two "Rules" she gave me when she invited me to live with her for the summer in Provincetown. She insisted her mom had paid for a condo on the beach ages ago and that she'd love to have me stay with her for the whole summer.

"Come! It will be the best summer ever. And you'll make so much more money waiting tables there than you would at home. I promise. Ten times more fun <u>and</u> more money. This is a total no-brainer, E."

I didn't want to do my usual overthinking and wanted to shout "Yes, I'll come" but didn't get it out before Alex added the disclaimer of, "I'd <u>love</u> for you to come, but I want to be straight with you: This summer will be anything but straight. We work hard and we play hard in Province-town, and it gets pretty wild when we play."

I was no stranger to Alex's late nights and one night stands, so I felt like I knew what she meant, but I wanted to make sure. "How wild?" I asked, nervous but excited, trying to seem cooler than I felt inside.

"Wild." She gave me that irresistible Alex smile before adding, "But don't worry. I'll be there at every step to show you the way. Plus, it's not like it's my boarding school friends or anything. You'll be fine. I won't let anything happen to you. And I <u>know</u> you can handle it. I wouldn't invite you otherwise. And you will LOVE it. I promise you, it will change your life, in the <u>best</u> of ways."

"I'll come."

"Wait, what? Are you serious?"

"Yes."

"Don't you want to think about it? Make your standard pros and cons lists?"

"No. I'm coming."

"Should you ask your dad?"

"He'll be OK with it. I'm almost twenty. I've been gone all year."

"Don't you want to hear the Rules first?"

"No. Wait. Yes. No," I laughed, getting giddy as I wrapped my head around the thought of heading to Provincetown for the summer with Alex and the crazy cast of characters I had imagined for months.

"Of course you do, my little rule lover."

I tossed a throw-pillow from my bed onto the futon where she was sitting. "Enough making fun of me. What are the Rules?"

"OK. There are only two." She cleared her voice theatrically, held her hands like she was reading from a real document, and made her voice sound official. "Rule number one: Whenever there's a choice between sleep and something really fun, we will ask ourselves, 'What will we remember in ten years? Getting sleep? Or the memories we'll make tonight?' The answer will be obvious. Rule number one is that fun wins. Every. Damn. Time."

"Umm...yeah...I've been living with this Rule since I met you in October. What's the second one?"

"OK," she laughed before resuming her official-sounding voice. "Rule number two: We swim _every_ morning. And if we were drunk the night before then we allocate extra time for _full_ submersion for a _full_ twenty minutes to naturally detox our bodies."

I looked at her skeptically.

"I looked it up online. It's a real thing."

"Sure it is, Alex."

"What? It is!"

"OK. Either way, I'm in."

Little did I know that we'd be doing the full twenty-minute submersion _every_ morning. Although I should've just assumed. I'd shaved years off my life trying to keep up with her since I met her. Or, maybe I'd added years by having enough fun that, at times, it almost felt like I could outrun the memory of Rob and forget that Mom bailed on me.

Alex cranked at a pace that demanded endurance and tolerance. I did my best to keep up, but was usually a few steps behind. My last night in Provincetown was no exception. When we walked into The Old Atlantic bar that final night, I gave myself a silent, symbolic pat-on-the-back for a stellar entrance.

The front door of the tiny place sits right on Commercial Street, so for a number of reasons, including the floor's sloping angle and the overall dim lighting, it's hard to tell who's in there until you walk in and your eyes adjust to the darkness of the place, whether it be night or day. Be careful on that slanting floor as you take the twenty steps between the front door and the bar. Once you get your drink, if you do snag a table, be ready for it to be as uneven as the floors. You can spot a rookie when their beer slides off the table.

Luckily, I had Alex to guide me past all rookie moves. She explained long before we arrived that "...it's all about the entrance. Aside from the exit, it's the most significant part of the night. With the exit, at least there are mitigating factors, like *Who you're leaving with?* And *Can one or both of you stand?* There are potential excuses. But you own your entrance for the night and you only get one chance to nail it.

"When you walk in, it's important to survey the scene, so long as you don't look like you're doing it. Look too hard and you seem self-conscious, scurrying to see who's in the room. Yet, you also don't want to seem like you lack the confidence to take a cool, long gaze around, like you're sizing up the night's potential."

"Who knew you cared what people thought?"

"I don't. It's not about what others think. It's more about setting the tone for the night; for the summer." She smiled and shook her head. "I have so much to show you, my friend. And I will."

And she did. Every night that summer was as much fun as she promised it would be. But what she didn't promise – what she didn't even mention, but what ended up being the biggest surprise; the biggest gift of the summer – was our first ten days there.

"It's a seasonal spot, Elizabeth, so we'll have some time to explore in the first couple weeks before we get really busy. I'll show you a different, special spot every day. We'll do a top 10 list and bang one out each morning."

"Wait, we're drinking every morning?"

"I don't know if I'm flattered or insulted that you assume all I want to do is party."

"Well..." and we both laughed.

"I think that's why I love it here so much. Behind all the partying, there are so many pockets of peace in Provincetown.

Places that I escape to throughout the summer, on days off from work, or between shifts. Mostly places to swim. Or sit. To be alone. To recharge without anyone needing, or expecting, anything from me. And I'll show you right away because, soon, our time together will be limited once the summer schedule kicks in."

She was right. Whenever I'd get a bit of time alone, which was rare with how many shifts I worked and how many beach parties I raged at; but when I did get some quiet, alone time, I'd make sure I got to one of those "special spots." I'd spend just enough time to feel restored. Just enough time before I started remembering too much.

I stayed in the present that whole summer. I refused to look behind me, or ahead. I promised Alex, and myself, that I'd live for each day. And I did. Plus, I made a ton of money. It was better than I could've imagined, all the way around. Yet, even though I was sad it'd be over the next day, I was still ready for bed on my final night in Provincetown when Alex said, "It's your last night in town, and I only have two more. We are <u>not</u> going to bed early, Elizabeth."

"Early? Alex, the only way it can be considered 'early' is the fact that it's already <u>early</u>-morning. I need some sleep."

"The <u>last</u> thing you need is sleep on your last night here. Come on, just one more beer on the beach out front. Who knows when we'll have this time again? I'm off to London for the semester."

"You'll be back in four months," I tried to shut her down before she made a solid closing case, like she always did. I was too late.

"I know that's the plan, Elizabeth, but who <u>really</u> knows what life will bring our way? Not me. Not you. Nobody. We have NOW. That's it. What's one more beer? In ten years are you going to remember being tired on your way home to Wellbury tomorrow, or are you going to remember us sitting on the beach, laughing under the stars?"

"Alright, alright. Let me grab a sweatshirt. ONE beer, Alex. One!"

She jumped up joyously. "Yes! Let's go!"

Of course, twenty minutes turned into an hour before I knew it.

And, of course, it was worth it. It always was. Usually co-workers from The Harbor Club joined us and I loved it when Jodi brought her guitar and James brought some beer, as both usually did. We'd sit on the beach, drinking and making up stupid songs about our day and the annoying people we waited on. The first night we did it, I figured the song that Jodi and James came up with *was* their best stuff, but every night they just got better and better. When they said they'd take it on the road someday, I didn't doubt it. I also didn't doubt Alex when she said she'd go with them.

I've always wondered how people could live like that. So in their dreams that logic went out the window. That the day-to-day stresses didn't stop or paralyze them. Instead, they created rituals like morning swims to begin each day anew; to let the water rinse away the doubt, fear, and uncertainty of life. To choose a new beginning, each day, free from regret, shame, and worry.

Mom could do that. She was a bird that couldn't be caged. And as much as it ruffled Dad's feathers, you couldn't help but be in love with her flight. Her joy for life.

Alex too.

I could never be like Alex. I could never just be in the moment. Never. But I came closest when I was with her. I dreaded saying goodbye, especially after such an incredible summer, but I reminded myself that space from Alex wasn't a bad thing. By the end of the previous semester, I was pretty stressed out trying to juggle Alex's party pace with my academic ambitions. In March, when midterm grades came out, I was questioning her influence on my life and even my decision to go to Provincetown. I feared I'd be in over my head without the structure of school to support our socializing. But it was the exact opposite. It's like, without the pressures of school, it was a more joyful, purer fun with Alex. That summer felt like the best version of what life could be.

I was feeling all the feels yesterday morning when I had to leave, after we swam. Alex was unusually motivated for her day off and said she was taking off as I started packing. "I'm going to walk the breakwater and hit The Point for the day. The crew might take the shuttle over later and meet me. Everyone's pretty much off from 2 p.m. on."

The Point was the only spit of land that I loved almost as much as I loved Blue Sky. It was similar in that it was remote and only people in-the-know could get to it. We'd spent the saltiest Sundays out at The Point that summer, "sunning, swimming, and swilling," as Alex always said.

"Ugh. That kills me. I <u>so</u> don't want to leave." It literally hurt my chest to think of them all at the beach together without me. The summer ending in a couple hours was tough to take.

I tried to get busy packing because Alex hates crying and hugging, so I didn't want to do the first or force the second. But she came over and stopped what I was doing. "Let's rip the bandage off and do this quickly," she said as she hugged me. And I swear her voice cracked, but I can't be sure. She'd never admit it, even if it did.

As we hugged goodbye that morning in Provincetown, and I thought of her being away in London that fall semester, I tried to feel less sad by reminding myself that I'd only known her for ten months. But that wasn't comforting at all because it brought back those weeks at school before we met. When I was me "After" the incident. When I was torn apart.

SATURDAY

Chapter Five

The sounds of Dad's cappuccino machine ripped me from my half-asleep state and dumped me into the present. My heart broke and my rage spiked all over again as I replayed what happened last night in Dad's office over and over in my mind on an endless loop.

I had flicked the light back on, feeling like a little kid about to do something naughty. The mature part of me knew that I should've just left it alone and given Dad his privacy, but the kid in me won and I had to check it out. I promised myself I wouldn't snoop. I wouldn't go into his private stuff. Just a quick glance into it – I'd always wondered what was in there. Dad would never tell me, other than it was "full of private things," which only made me want to know more.

In middle school, we learned about the dangers of guns at home. A visiting police officer said that sometimes parents keep guns in closets, which was the most dangerous thing to do. But even guns in safes could still be dangerous. The thought of a gun in Dad's safe terrified me.

"Dad, is there a gun in your safe?" I asked when he picked me up from school that day.

"No, Honey. Why would you think that?"

"A police officer said there might be. What about in your closet?"

"No, Honey. There are no guns in the house. I don't own a gun."

That appeased me, but while we were on the topic and he seemed to be so forthcoming in the moment, I asked, "What _is_ in the safe, Dad?"

"Private things."

"Like what?"

"That's what makes it private. It's not to share." He smiled and tousled my hair.

"Can I have a safe of private things?"

"No."

"Why not?"

"Because you're too young to keep things private from me."

"That's not fair."

"Someday you'll see that it is, in fact, very fair."

"OK. But, why <u>don't</u> you have a gun in that safe? Don't you want to protect me?"

"Sweet Girl, I'd do <u>anything</u> to protect you. Anything. Guns have nothing to do with that."

Those words echoed in my head as I approached the safe, still surprised that it was actually open and equally curious about its contents. I knew I should've turned around, walked away, and flicked the light off for the night. But I just couldn't help myself.

Once I was in front of it, I saw a few small boxes, a handful of files, some binders. I didn't want to snoop any further. It was enough already. I was about to turn away when the color blue caught my eye.

In the safe, standing upright and facing out, were two long, blue envelopes.

When I saw the handwriting, my heart started singing an old song I hadn't heard in years but knew every beat, build, and lyric, from start to finish.

My hand reached for them before my head registered what I was doing.

With shaking hands, I flipped between the two envelopes.

One to Dad.

One to Me.

Both were torn open and dated the month she left.

For a moment, I was outside my body, looking at myself. My heart and mind were racing while I stood completely still, rooted to my place in front of Dad's safe.

As I started to process what I had in my hands, they shook.

In all the ways I pictured Mom reentering my life, and how I'd feel about it, I never figured that she'd try to get to me and that Dad would block it.

How could he?

I NEVER imagined that he'd do this. It NEVER crossed my mind. Ever.

Before my rage took over, I snapped into action. Dad could wake up at any moment. I had to act fast in whatever I was going to do.

But, WHAT WOULD I DO?

I forced myself to focus.

Of course, I needed to take the letters. They were mine. Well, one was. But, fuck Dad, at this point, weren't they both mine?

I had to at least read them.

I clutched them to my chest as I ran out of Dad's office and upstairs to my room where I sat in the window nook, trying to control the white-hot rage simmering within me as I tried to think of how Dad, my hero and foundation, could do this to me.

He <u>must</u> have reasons for not sharing them with me.

For keeping them, but keeping them from me.

He must.

But what the hell could they be?

Maybe I shouldn't read them. Maybe he was protecting me from whatever was in them by not giving them to me.

But...I had to read them.

I started with the one addressed to Dad. I pulled out the letter, took a deep breath, and somehow steadied my hands enough to read.

Mike,

How dare you?

You have sunk to a new low and it might be one we don't rise from.

You are selfish, scared, and small.

You are cold and calculating.

Imagine my surprise and subsequent embarrassment to learn upon arriving at school pickup today that you dismissed Elizabeth a couple hours earlier.

Imagine my fear as I called your phone and was sent directly to voicemail.

Imagine the worry as I wove in and out of traffic, racing home because, surely, something was wrong for you to do this.

Imagine my fury when I read your note that you and Elizabeth snuck off for a weekend getaway.

Would it have killed you to let me give Elizabeth a proper "Goodbye"?

Could you not see beyond your own insecurity to do anything other than act selfish?

All I wanted was to go to the artists' retreat for 30 days.

All of it was planned.

All it would've taken is for you to see me – to really see me – and say, "Go. I know you need this."

How could you cancel the support I lined up from Alice and the Owens?

How can you justify that, when they shuffled their lives to help?

How can you play God like this?

After today, I have zero doubts that I need to do this; that I need to break away from you, for my own sanity.

After today, you have shown me everything I need to see to leave feeling unguilty.

Yes, I'm heartbroken to leave without saying a goodbye to Elizabeth; but

Yes, I trust my bond with her is bigger than your betrayal; and that

Yes, she will be sad that I'm gone, but will be better for it when I come back more myself.

If you have any sense of compassion – if you love our daughter, which I know you do – then please give her the letter I'm including for her.

Let me leave somewhat on my terms after robbing me of the chance to do it fully my way.

Please make it right and give this to her.

As for you and me, I have very little to say that hasn't been said – or shouted – in the last few years. I'm so sick of hearing myself say the same things; you must be too.

In some ways, I envisioned a tearful goodbye between us, with me apologizing for needing to leave for this retreat; and letting you know I forgive you for what you did.

But I don't feel any of that right now, which makes leaving easier. So, thank you for that, Mike.

I can't help it if I'm me. I see the world one way, and you see it another. I see blue skies ahead where you see potential squalls. I want to live by embracing beauty, you want to live in a bunker. I can't let Elizabeth live that way. She needs to dream. To love. To not to be scared of herself. Or anyone. I need to do this so she can know who I truly am and, hopefully, that <u>she</u> can become <u>whoever</u> she wants to. And, hopefully, it will be someone who runs towards life, not away from it.

I'll see you and E. in 30 days.

No longer yours,
Evangeline

I couldn't formulate a clear thought.

See you and E. in 30 days?

What the fuck happened?

I willed my shaking hands to steady so I didn't rip anything as I pulled out my letter.

Dearest, Elizabeth.

My Girl.

I hope you had a fantastic adventure with Dad.

I'm going on an adventure, too; an art adventure!

I'll be at a cool camp in the woods with other artists.

We'll create art all day and all night.

It will be great,

EXCEPT,

That I can't bring you with me, and

The camp is for 30 sleeps, and

I can't have visitors or letters or phone calls or anything.

But I can write, so I will. Every day.

I will miss you terribly.

My Girl, please know my heart will always be with you,

as will my spirit and all my strength.

I have all the confidence in the world that you'll be OK,

without me, for this short time,

because when I return, I'll be less preoccupied,

and even better.

For you. For me.

Until then, Elizabeth, know that I love you.

I love you.

I love you.

I love you.

Forever and ever, I love you.

I know that I have been distracted these last few months,

but know that, when I return, I'll be there for you,

for the rest of your Life.

For now, remember, the sky we look at is the same.

All my love,

Mom

I stared at her drawing on the back of my letter for so long that the blues in her night sky actually started swirling with the silver and gold stars so they dazzled off the page.

I sat there, dumbfounded.

How could Dad keep this from me?

How could he make me think she just took off and <u>never</u> returned without one word?

Did she write to me every day like she said she would?

Where were those letters?

I tiptoed back downstairs to peer into the safe again, carefully shuffling things to try to find more letters, or anything, from her. Nothing. I wanted to look through every document and file and envelope in Dad's office and bedroom to make sure, but my heart was in my throat; I was so nervous Dad would wake up and find me. I wasn't ready for a confrontation. Yet.

I tried to sleep on it but sleep was impossible. I tossed and turned and, a few times, even got up to rage into Dad's room, wake him up from a sound sleep, and demand answers. But every time I was up and on my way to his room, my mind started spinning. I figured there was more to this than I was seeing, and I should think a bit more about how to handle it.

In the light of day the next morning, I knew what I had to do. I threw on my robe and slippers, and charged downstairs with the letters, ready to confront him.

When I got downstairs, I was met with a note:

Good morning, Sweet Girl.
I'm sorry that I had to leave so early.

I'll look forward to seeing you at the barbeque later.

Have a great day!

Love, Dad

The confrontation would have to wait. I tried to call him, but as expected, his phone's "Do Not Disturb" was on like it always was for long trips. Dad, so predictable. Except, not at all.

I started doing laps around the kitchen island as my mind outpaced my legs. I couldn't stop the swirling of emotions and questions. I was too wired to sleep. It was too early to drink. The only thing left to keep my sanity was to run.

Chapter Six

Ithrew on my running shoes, found *Shake It Off* on my iPod, and hit the streets. I went right instead of left to avoid running past Ruth's house.

It was cool for an August morning, but I welcomed the chill and found my pace right away. Cruising by familiar yards should've been comforting, but felt discomforting because none of it had changed, while so much of me had.

Everyone still had the same, lush, perfectly symmetrical yards and plantings. Most homes still had the same SUVs parked in their driveways. Thankfully, none of my neighbors were in their yards or I would've felt the need to do the obligatory, *How have you been?* Bullshit. I didn't want to chitchat with Dad, Gloria, or Ruth and The Millers, let alone relative strangers. I was on high-alert to avoid situations where I was expected to share. And even if Gloria hadn't asked me to sleep over in years, I was on-edge, waiting for the potential offer.

When she first moved to Wellbury and bought her condo, all she could talk about was how I had a room there. She <u>insisted</u> that I help her decorate so I'd feel comfortable at her place. I knew she was trying hard, but it was too hard, and it drove me nuts.

The only time I'd ever seen Gloria cry was when I was about thirteen, after a few years of her endless sleepover invites (despite my consistent declines) and calling her guest room "Elizabeth's Room" (despite my consistent corrections).

Looking back, I don't know why it mattered to me so much that we didn't call it my room. I don't know it mattered to her so much that we did.

One day, I had had enough and yelled, "It's <u>not</u> my room. I don't have a room here. I have <u>one</u> room. At my house. With my Dad. I don't <u>need</u> a room here. You're not my mother. I shouldn't have a room here."

Quietly, she said, "OK, Elizabeth. I won't bring it up again. I'm sorry I keep pushing it."

I felt self-righteous, having won the battle. But then she excused herself and I heard her start crying before she got to her room and shut the door.

She never called it my room, or suggested a sleepover, again.

* * * *

Running still had the power to clear my mind. The lull of it that day made me lose my direction so much so that I didn't realize what neighborhood I was in until I looked up and stopped dead in my tracks.

Rob's old cottage colony – A place that had always intrigued me as a kid because it was its own little village surrounded by spruce trees, not a mile from the coast.

I leaned forward, putting my hands on my knees as I tried to catch my breath. I was fighting for air as I stood there, glued to that horrendous spot. All I could do was stay bent as I battled for breath. I tried to take long, slow draws of air as I willed the images away, but once they started, they pulled me back to the night that gave me a new "Before" and "After" to judge my life by.

I hardly recognized the "Before" me who was excitedly applying more makeup than usual, wearing a short black dress that Ruth would've <u>never</u> approved of, and already planning how to sneak a drink for liquid courage to talk to Rob at the barbeque. I was heading there without Ruth for the first time because her freshman orientation had started. I was ready for a fun night. I had graduated from high school, was almost over my Brendan heartbreak and ten pounds lighter because of it, and feeling very grown up "Before."

I didn't know Rob until he started working for Dad as a lawn mower. We went to the same school, but he was a senior when I was a freshman, and, even if we were in the same grade, we still wouldn't have known each other. Rob was an All-Star athlete in every sport he played which made him cool and, alas, I was not. Especially freshman year.

Rob only lasted a couple years at college when he came back to Wellbury and started working for Dad full time and quickly moved from lawn mower to salesperson where he started making Dad more money. When Rob's parents moved to Texas not long after he returned to Wellbury, Rob stayed behind and told Dad he was committed to growing the business with him. Dad started relying on Rob more, which meant he was around more, which only made me crush harder.

Towards the end of my senior year, our interactions got more and more flirtatious. He started telling me how beautiful I was, which boys my age didn't do. Even Brendan didn't throw out as many, "Elizabeth, you look beautiful today," as Rob did. And since Brendan had broken my heart not long before Rob started paying more attention to me, I was like a sponge for it. He asked questions about what I wanted to do when I got older. He joked that Brendan wasn't good enough for me, and that he'd be happy to show me what a "Real Man" was like. I'd laugh, flattered. And so it went. It was all harmless enough.

Until last summer.

Until a couple days before the barbeque when Rob came into the conference room at Dad's office and cranked up the flirting. I was there watching *Flashdance* on my laptop, waiting for Dad. I tried to act cool, calm, and collected while hoping my heart didn't literally pop out of my chest, which felt like a real possibility.

"Where's your sidekick? Rita?"

"Ruth." (She'd HATE that he didn't know her name, though she wouldn't admit she cared.)

"Right, Ruth. Usually she's around, preventing me from flirting with you by shooting eye daggers at me that are so sharp, I can really feel them."

I almost snorted from laughing so unexpectedly. "Ha. She means well."

"She's boring," he said with a huge smile so it didn't seem cruel but just factual. I ignored the insult.

"Well, she already left for school. I'm next. I leave next week."

"That's right. Your dad said you leave soon. I hope that doesn't mean you won't be at the barbeque this year."

"I'll be there."

"Great. I won't even pretend that I'm not looking forward to shamelessly flirting without Ruth there."

"We'll see." And then I channeled every "Cool Girl" vibe I could muster and turned back to my laptop, leaving him standing in the doorway. I nailed it.

"Yes, we'll see. See you at the barbeque, Elizabeth," he said.

"See you." I managed to keep my voice the same pitch despite my giddiness.

That's what's hard for me to wrap my head around. How it all went so badly so quickly.

The barbeque was fun. Until it wasn't.

Rob was a perfect gentleman. Until he wasn't.

I was in control. Until I wasn't.

The barbeque was rowdy that year. I walked into a huge warehouse with a DJ in the corner spinning 90s hip hop, and helped myself on the down-low to the circular, help-yourself bar with rum, tequila, vodka, and local beer. I chose rum and no one seemed to notice. The men were dressed in button-down shirts minus the tie. The women all wore cocktail dresses. But Rob stood out from the rest in a pressed navy suit that looked like an ad from *GQ* magazine. I took my first drink down in a few gulps to settle my nerves and hid the cup, even though I felt mature and ready to enjoy Dad's party in a new way, now that I wasn't a high-schooler.

I was a mere week from going away, on my own. I felt perfectly happy and fully confident; I felt like I had finally arrived in my own life. I wasn't even really sneaking the cocktails after that first one, which only emboldened me. I felt like an adult at an adult party. And it was a massive party, bigger than ever since Dad's business and team had nearly doubled that year. He hired the DJ instead of blasting a playlist that Jane, his assistant, usually made. People were dancing, which had never happened. I was having a blast, buzzed on booze and Rob's attention. He was working the room, being professional as he chatted with colleagues and clients, but I could feel him watching me from a distance and I loved it. We made eye contact whenever we could and found reasons to meet up in the corners to laugh and flirt.

I kept drinking a lot. Like, a lot, A LOT. I was slamming Captain & Cokes as fast as I could get them. I haven't had one since that night because even a whiff of spiced rum makes me gag. Thank God my tolerance for the smell of Coke is better, though it still surprises me how poignant a smell Coke has. Who knew or noticed? Not me, until "After."

Rob, on the other hand, was on-the-clock as Designated Driver until the very end of the party when we sat outside so he could slam a few drinks quickly.

I wish I had not tried to keep up at that point, but we were full-on flirting and I was keen to stay loose and keep it going. As he slugged back a couple cocktails, I matched him drink-for-drink, and we plotted our escape.

This is where it gets fuzzy.

He insisted that we not tell anyone we were hanging out. I agreed, but wasn't as worried about it as he was. Regardless, we decided I'd tell Dad that I was leaving for a "Going Away" party for a few classmates, and then Rob would meet me outside.

I guess we were lucky we left before I started getting visibly wasted. Or, that was the not-so-lucky part. Maybe if those final drinks had caught up with me thirty minutes sooner or, even as I was saying goodbye, then I would've been more obviously sloshed and Dad or Gloria would've intervened and said, "You're not going anywhere but home, young lady."

When we got to my car, I tried to walk him backwards and kiss him, but I stumbled and he caught me.

"Whoa, easy. Let's get you out of here."

"Whoops!" I heard myself slur. Those last few drinks were hitting me hard, "I don't feel great."

"Let's go to my cottage for a bit. It's early. You'll feel better soon."

He told me to drive my car to his place and he'd drive his.

I had a flash of, "This is a <u>bad</u> idea," but ignored it.

As I drove, I wanted to call him to bail, but I didn't have his number.

I was starting to feel physically sick pretty quickly and considered pulling over to throw up, but knew that wasn't safe. I figured I'd follow him to his place, explain that I was too sick to hang, and ask him to drive me home. I'd deal with my car the next day. Dad wouldn't love it, but he'd understand.

At that point, I naively thought I could walk away from the whole thing unscathed, even though, the further we got from the party atmosphere, the closer I was to realizing how WASTED I actually was.

I wanted to go home. I <u>needed</u> to go home.

All those Captain & Cokes were sloshing around my stomach and, by the time we pulled into his parking spots, I got out of my car, took two steps away from it, and hurled in the bushes. The spruces started spinning.

Where was I?

Who was rubbing my back?

"Let's get you inside to rest," Rob said.

I wanted to stay outside. I wanted to call Dad.

"I need to call my dad and tell him to come get me," I managed to get out.

"We already texted him and told him you're staying at Tina's. Don't you remember? We did that outside."

We did?

Blackness.

He lifted my face off the toilet bowl and told me to brush my teeth.

I didn't want to brush my teeth.

Why did I have to? I thought.

I just wanted to go back to sleep.

The toilet seat was fine. Just leave me alone.

No, I don't want to take my dress off.

I'm fine. I just want to take a nap.

"Will you call my dad to come get me?" I slurred.

No? OK. I guess I'll just take a quick nap and then I'll be sober to drive home.

And then I must have passed out. Dreams I can't remember. Thoughts of driving home. My own room, my own bed...and the soft yellow wallpaper that... Suddenly I woke up.

What was happening? What was inside me? Who is this? Wait...what?

I felt his hot breath on my neck.

WAIT.

WHAT THE FUCK...?

Who was inside of me?

Was someone inside of me?

I needed to wake up from this nightmare.

"Wait, hold on. I'm awake and I don't want this," I said.

His grunting in my ear.

"Hold on. Wait..." I said again.

What time was it?

Where were we?

"Rob, STOP!" I shouted.

I just said that out loud, right?

"Rob. Wait!" I tried again.

"Oh good, you're awake now," he said with a smile totally void of a human being.

"What...? You knew...?"

I felt sick as I squirmed beneath him.

I needed to WAKE UP. This couldn't be happening.

"What the FUCK, Rob?"

I started to cry.

To buck.

To push him away from me.

His full weight on top of me was too heavy.

I balled my fists and started pounding, trying to land on his face but mostly hitting his shoulders.

He pinned my arms back. "I'm almost done. Just go back to sleep."

I screamed.

He used one hand to cover my mouth.

I tried to bite.

"You little bitch. Just fucking relax."

Spit landed on my face, mixing with my tears and snot.

I couldn't get a solid bite, but I couldn't stop trying.

He grabbed a pillow and put it over my face.

"Just settle down. This is happening one way or the other. You're only prolonging it. Trust me, I've had it go both ways, and it's always better when the bitch just gives up and lets me finish. I'll be done soon."

I wouldn't stop fighting.

"I'm not trying to kill you. Just have some fun. Relax. Let me finish," he said to the pillow covering my face. My heart rate skyrocketed. I tried not to choke on my sobs.

I realized at some point, somehow, that I wasn't getting out from under him. That the quickest way to end this would be to just go limp.

To go to another place mentally.

To disassociate.

I processed that. And that's what I did.

I went limp.

I detached my mind from my body. Instead of thinking about what was happening, I pictured myself floating through blackness, no longer there; being carried calmly by forces I couldn't see but felt.

As soon as I did, it was over in a few pumps.

He pulled the pillow away and said, "See, you enjoyed it. I knew you would."

He pulled out of me and jumped off the bed, seemingly sober and happy.

I scrambled up to the headboard, trying to pull myself into myself as he got up, walked into the bathroom, threw a towel at me, and shut the door.

I pulled my dress down and spotted my flip-flops and purse by the door. All I needed was my underwear. I was about to leave them behind when I saw them in the far corner. I tried to spring from the bed to my underwear, but fell face forward on the bed's corner, busting my lip. I screamed out in pain.

"Is everything OK out there?" he yelled as he flushed the toilet.

In one motion, I grabbed my underwear, jumped up, ran towards the door, scooped up my bag and shoes, and ran to my car. I was pulling out by the time he was at the door yelling, "Come back! We need to clear some things up!"

I drove as fast as I could, looking behind to make sure he wasn't following me.

When I knew I was far enough away, I pulled over to the side of the road and sobbed.

Chapter Seven

Last year, the morning after the barbeque, I sat with the phone in my hand for what felt like hours, trying to work up the courage to call Ruth and just get the words out. But I couldn't. It's like, whenever I thought I had the words, they'd plummet to the bottom of my stomach and just sit there, like an immovable rock. I convinced myself that I was doing her a favor by not calling. That it was selfish to tell her and ruin her first week at school. In our brief, excited chats since she arrived at Vassar, it sounded like she loved her roommate, and was making friends.

I was supposed to be next. Off to my next chapter. Off to live my best life.

But living life felt like too tall an order.

How could I live when it felt like a part of me had died that night with Rob?

I wasn't myself. My full self. My old self. I missed her.

I was pissed at her.

I loved her.

I felt sorry I couldn't protect her.

I thought of telling Dad, but I just couldn't deal with him knowing. The thought of that made my chest constrict until it was hard to breathe.

It was all so physically painful that I just wanted to get out of my body. Just leave it. Yet, in some ways, on some level, I thought that I deserved that pain. I mean, why did I get that drunk? Why did I lose control like that? Why was I sneaking around? Lying to Dad? Why didn't I follow the rules?

I knew I didn't ask for it, but I let it happen.

And for that, I didn't know how I'd ever forgive myself.

Instead of telling anyone, when I got home to Dad's that night, I walked slowly upstairs, kicked off my shoes, threw my clothes to the floor and showered. I trashed everything I had been wearing deep down in the garbage where Dad wouldn't find it.

And then I shoved the memory of what had happened deep down where I wouldn't find it.

I told Dad my busted lip was from opening my car door too aggressively by accident. I got Pepto pills for the heartburn and blamed pre-college stress for the lack of appetite. And then I played that anxiety card for the rest of the week, right up until Dad and Gloria dropped me off at school when I averted big hugs by saying that I was afraid

I'd start bawling and not be able to stop, so we'd just make it a wave and a "See you later."

And then I did what I did that night in Rob's bed; I disassociated. I went to another place. It worked once to survive. I hoped it would work again.

When stray thoughts like, *Did he use a condom? Am I pregnant? Do I have an STD?* assaulted me, I shielded myself before they could truly penetrate my consciousness. I simply refused to acknowledge them. And I waited.

And that worked.

Mostly.

Until it didn't have to anymore.

Until I met Alex in Dr. Rogers' class.

* * * *

I finally caught my breath. There were bikes and boogie boards scattered in the yard by the new summer tenants. I tried to be comforted by new memories being made there, but seeing it as a happy place only made me feel sadder.

I pulled myself away from Rob's old cottage, and started walking back to my house. The pep in my step was long gone and I couldn't restart my jog no matter what playlist I tried. The morning's chilly sunshine was turning cloudy quickly, mirroring how I felt: dark and stormy. It felt like I'd been in a battle. And I was so tired of fighting. But how could I stop?

For a split second, the answer seemed obvious: Strength in numbers. I could tell someone. I could share this shame, this burden. I could go talk to Ruth. I could walk up to her front door like I've done thousands of times, walk in without ringing the doorbell, go into her room, lay on her bed curled on my left side so I could look out the cool little octagon window that's at eye-level when laying there, and cry as I told her what happened.

It would be its own battle to get those words out. But I could. I could tell her.

It's not like I didn't think of telling her as soon as it happened. And then kept considering it in the minutes, hours, and days that followed. But I just couldn't bring myself to make the call. I couldn't find my voice to tell that chapter of my story. I wanted to rip it out instead.

My body, my heart, my head. It all hurt. And I just wanted Ruth.

That's not true. I wanted my mother. Mom. I ached for her. It was much sharper than the want I felt during graduation when I kept scanning the bleachers for her face, trying to tune out the mothers holding "Congratulations" banners and looking like they'd burst with pride. I wanted to believe she'd <u>finally</u> show up on the biggest milestone of my life to date, besides the day she left. But she wasn't there. It gutted me, and then I felt guilty about that. I felt ashamed for wanting more after my incredible, played-like-a-teen-movie-script "Senior Week." But I wanted more. I wanted Mom. But it was a want.

After Rob, it was an ache.

Not that it mattered what it was either time. She wasn't there.

Why did it feel like a slap across my face each and every time I realized that truth?

I rubbed my cheek subconsciously while I walked home.

The sky got darker and darker as I walked. A summer storm was brewing and I welcomed the idea of a rainy day because maybe I'd be able to just sleep until the barbeque when I could confront Dad. And Gloria. There was no way she didn't know about the letters. They told each other <u>everything</u>. As I thought about it, my anger ratcheted up. Them keeping this secret from me – in cahoots together, behind my back, about my mother – it made me so angry. It made me sick to my stomach.

I needed to vent. I needed to talk to <u>someone</u>. I grabbed my phone and dialed Alex. Maybe I'd catch her before she boarded her plane to London.

It rang and rang. Just when I was about to hang up and shoot her a "NBD" text, she answered. "Hey! I just got through security. I'm on my way!"

"Oh, OK."

"Well, actually, I have a minute. I'm through security. I think my flight leaves in a while. I have to look. What's up? How was the ride back? Sorry I didn't call you last night. We went pretty hard and then, as expected, I was hustling to get on the road this morning because I underestimated how much I had to clean."

"I told you I would've helped more!"

"Stop! That's <u>not</u> what I'm saying. I had people over last night. We destroyed the place. Us cleaning before would've been pointless. It's all good."

"OK..."

"It's all good. Relax, E. Jesus, you're already wound back up tighter than a goddamn top. You better not go back to your super uptight, no-fun, always-worried, sad self while I'm abroad. I better not come back and have to start over with you."

I wanted to laugh, and I did, but I didn't really feel it.

"Seriously, Elizabeth, is everything OK?"

"Eh, it hasn't been a good trip home so far."

"What? How can that be? It hasn't even been a full twenty-four hours, has it?"

"I know."

"What happened?"

What could I say? I had barely shown Alex any emotion about my mother, so where would I start? Did I start with Brendan's engagement and then go blow-by-blow until I just found myself crumbled in front of Rob's old cottage? It was all swirling in my head, but all I came up with was, "Nothing. Well, I mean, I don't know."

"OK, E. But you don't sound like nothing's wrong."

"Brendan's getting married," is the first thing that came out.

"Wait, what? It's hard to hear you above this airport noise. What'd you say?"

"Brendan's getti...never mind. What I really called about was that I just found these letters from my..."

Blaring in the background, I heard, "Final boarding call for Flight 523 to Heathrow..."

"Shit! I guess my plane leaves <u>now</u>. I gotta go."

"Shit. OK."

"I'm sorry, but if I don't hang up and sprint, I'm gonna miss this flight. I love you. I'll call when I can so you can tell me what's going on. OK? I love you! Talk in a few!" And then she was gone.

I sat for a moment with the phone in my hand. Maybe it was for the best that she couldn't talk. Sometimes her laissez-faire attitude was contagious and fun, but sometimes it was offensive and rude, depending on what mood I was in, or what kind of advice I really wanted to hear. And then, sometimes, she was anything but laissez-faire and wanted to dig deep with intense questioning, like the night I told her about Mom leaving.

It was the first Monday night of my life that I was drinking and we were sitting on her bed, sharing a bottle of Two-Buck Chuck wine, listening to Ed Sheeran, and working on our assignments for Dr. Rogers' class. When I told her that I wasn't sure why Mom up-and-left, she wouldn't leave it alone, making me feel stupid, like Tina did a couple years before, that I didn't know why I was left behind.

"But that makes no sense. Like, <u>why</u> did she leave?"

"Because she wanted other things in life."

"There's more to it. There has to be. What did your dad say when you asked him?"

"We don't really talk about it."

"Why not? Aren't you curious?"

"I never really ask him."

"Like often?"

"Like...ever," I said quietly. "I think it's too painful for him and, I mean, it is what it is. Right? Like, why does the reason matter?" I tried to sound like I meant what I was saying.

"Of course the reason matters. That's nuts to think it doesn't."

"I don't know...I mean, I did ask once..."

"OK, what did he say?"

"He said she left to be happier, basically."

"Why? Was your Dad a dick? You always make him sound so great. And you're great. So, like, what else did she want?"

"I don't know."

"And you're OK with that? You don't have a million questions? I can think of two million in two minutes."

I just started crying and, since it was the second time of only two times that I've cried in front of her, my tears stopped her dead in her tracks.

"Shit! E! What's wrong?"

"I don't know…" I didn't know how to tell her that, I wasn't even really crying because Mom left. I had shed so many buckets of those tears that they ran dry. I was crying for myself. That I never thought to ask Dad, unless prompted by a super curious friend. To really push him for answers. That I just accepted it all. That I didn't care enough about what I needed to upset Dad any more than he already was.

But how could I tell Alex that? She wouldn't get it. She didn't spend time thinking of what family members she might upset because there were none around. Even though Mom left me, I still had Dad. Alex didn't have anyone stable growing up. She was always trying to get someone's attention.

Elle, her mother, insisted that Alex start calling her Elle after Alex's father died. When I asked why, Alex just shrugged her shoulders like it was no big deal and said, "She didn't ever want kids so she was in denial about it. She thought it would be more fun – for her – if we pretended that we were sisters instead of mother and daughter. I didn't care. I went along with it. It was actually a riot."

That made me sad. For both of them.

When she was barely fourteen, Alex asked if she could go to boarding school, and then was excited, yet heartbroken, by how little convincing Elle needed to send her away. Alex claimed that being "shipped away at such a young age" was why she "thrived on being surrounded by friends 24x7."

She always painted boarding school as a non-stop adventure, and Elle's constant traveling and champagne breakfasts as entertaining. But, after a while, the stories sounded sad and lonely, if you listened long and close enough.

Alex didn't see it that way, or at least she didn't admit that she saw it that way. Yet…I don't know…sometimes I thought that somewhere, DEEP down, she wished she had a different childhood, even when convincing herself that it was wild, fantastic fun that she wouldn't trade for any treasure.

I know most people looked at her and only saw a spoiled party girl. And she was. But she was spoiled with money

<u>only</u>. Alex had zero spoiling with love. I'd seen beneath her armor and knew that it was as strong as it was because of how she was raised. Or, more accurately put: the way she lacked any raising at all.

Chapter Eight

Dear Mom,

I write in secret. To let you know I am not mad because you left even if I wish you did not but I can forgive you if you want to come get me now.

I know that Dad will be sad if I leave but maybe we can all live in the same town and get ice cream together sometimes.

I think we all love each other and that is what will be best. If you really, really, really think about it then you will think so too so come get me and I know we can explain it to Dad and he will understand and it will all be good again.

I will keep a bag packed under my bed so I am ready when you come and I will not be any trouble at all and I can adjust really easy and you will see that when you come get me.

I love you and I will see you soon and it will all be OK I promise.

Love, your daughter who is not mad I promise,

Elizabeth Joseph

I found that unsent letter while I rummaged through my desk last night before I went to sleep. I must've been six or seven when I wrote it, not too long after Mom left. I remember, when I finished, I asked Dad how I could send a letter, but didn't tell him it was for Mom. He explained that I'd need an address.

Later that night, I thought I was so smooth when I asked Dad, "Where do I find an address for someone?"

"It depends. There used to be something called a phone book that had everyone's addresses, but now people mostly ask each other, or some people can be found on the Internet."

I kept eating.

"Honey, do you want me to help you send a letter?"

I didn't know what to do. I needed his help, but didn't want to hurt his feelings.

"Honey, if you wrote your mom a letter, then…"

Tears started to stream down my face.

"Oh, Elizabeth, come here," and Dad turned his chair and opened his arms so I could pop up and into them.

"Honey, if you wrote Mom a letter, then I think that's completely understandable. And I wish I could help you send it to her. But, earlier, when I said we needed an address to send someone a letter…?"

I nodded, sniffling my snot.

"We don't have an address for Mom. She hasn't given us one yet. I don't know if she even has one. She might be still figuring out where to live, which is why we haven't heard from her."

"We have no way of finding her?"

"No, Honey, we don't."

I sat there, curled up in his arms, crying, for what felt like days. He kept subtly shifting me from knee to knee, but kept me fully encircled.

Later, he told me to keep the letter somewhere safe so we could send it if we ever got Mom's address. I kept it for all these years in a folder with a sixth-grade report on "What Dad Does," which was supposed to be about his job, but ended up being about him and Mom's love story, really.

I started the interview for that school assignment with, "Dad, when you were my age, what did you want to be when you grew up?" This was the question my fifth-grade teacher, Mrs. Powers, told us to start with, and then she told us the follow-up question was just as important, so mine was, "Why did (or didn't) you become that?"

"I wanted to be a horticulturist."

"A horti... what did you just say?"

He smiled, and I was aware at that moment that it had been a while since I saw him smile.

"A horticulturalist. Someone who studies plants and trees, basically. A scientist. And, actually, it's kind of part of the reason your mother and I were so drawn to each other at first."

"It was? Did she want to be a horticulaturalister too?"

"No, your mother always wanted to be an artist. But when we first started dating, back in Cambridge, when we were young and broke, before we made our way to New York, we spent our weekends going around Cambridge and Boston, looking in all the public gardens and as many private ones as we could get glimpses of, and we'd take photos and make sketches and then head home and talk about them. I'd research them, and write about them. Mom would paint them. We swore we'd write and illustrate a book someday. Long after we left Cambridge, we'd scour every city and town we visited for their gardens. We just couldn't give it up."

"Why did you then? Give up?"

Dad thought about it with a faraway look on his face before refocusing on me. "Well, we had to grow up, basically. We had to make some money. I decided I'd be a land-scaper. We started to think about moving. We got ready for you, Sweetheart. We did all the next, right things to do. <u>You</u> were the best thing we ever did."

"And, you still work with plants as a landscaper, so you did follow your dream. Didn't you, Dad?"

"I sure did."

That might've been the first lie he ever told me.

The grade on the report was a B and the comment from Mrs. Powers said, "Well written, but didn't stay close enough to the topic to earn a higher grade."

Normally, less than an A would've bothered me, but not this time. I was OK with the B. I had a story about Dad and Mom, before they started fighting, and before she left. That was worth so much more than an A. That school report, and the letter to Mom, were the only two paper memories of Mom that weren't burned the night of my fifteenth birthday when I realized that yet <u>another</u> birthday had come and gone without a word from her. It had been eight years and, for some reason, that number felt unacceptable to me.

I was sitting on my bed, reading through the cards I had from her and Dad before she left, because they were all in her handwriting. I was wondering what it is about me that made my own mother not want to acknowledge my birthday. I was looking around at my fifteenth birthday haul, including presents and cards from Dad, Gloria, and friends, but all I wanted was Mom. A card or a call, a lifeline to her. Some acknowledgement that she still thought of me. <u>Something.</u>

I felt awful.

Lower than low.

I started sobbing into the pillow because I didn't want Gloria to hear me. When she knocked on my door, I was horrified. I didn't want to admit that I was still crying about Mom. That felt even weaker than weak, which felt lower than the aforementioned low.

I didn't want to let her in, but she joked that, "It's the first time your father left me with you, so I have to be a pain in the ass if I hear you crying."

She had a point.

I opened the door and agreed to go talk to her on the couch.

As we talked, I started to feel – really feel – my rage towards Mom, my pent-up, long-overdue rage. I said, "I'm just so pissed at her." Then followed it up with, "I know I shouldn't be this mad still."

"You are entitled to feel however you feel. It's your life, on your terms, <u>whatever</u> those are for <u>you</u>. Try not to tell yourself how you should feel; just feel it. In your body, with your heart, not your head."

I could see why she had so many clients. I couldn't see why I'd never asked her for help before. Maybe life would've hurt less if I had just let her in all those years ago, when she first arrived. I tried not to focus on the past. I had her <u>now</u>.

"But that hurts too much." I trusted her enough to let my voice shake without trying to control it.

"I know. But it's the only way to heal. You have to go through it, not over it."

It was winter. The fire was roaring. We talked for a couple hours and, at the end, I just wanted to capture all those emotions and memories, and put them in a burlap sack and throw them overboard so they could fall to the depths of the sea and never come back to me. That wasn't possible, but as I sat in front of the fire, I realized what was.

I went upstairs and gathered what I had left of Mom: The cards and artwork she gave me before she left. All the photos I had of her, of us, of our family. A notebook I had been keeping to remind me of all the things I was sure she'd want the play-by-play on someday, like the day I learned to ride a bike, or my first Honor Roll certificate, first recital...all the things she missed that I knew she'd want to get back someday. But I no longer believed that so I added it to my pile that I brought downstairs with me.

I stood squarely in front of Gloria. "I want to put Mom behind me. I want to move on. I want to burn these things to set me free."

"If that's what you want, you're old enough to make these decisions, because you're old enough to realize that, once you toss all those things in the fire, they're gone for-ever. Just be sure. One-hundred-percent present. One-hun-dred-percent sure."

I stood there, rooted to the floor in front of the fire, my hands full of Mom. "I understand. I think it's some-thing I need to do."

"You think?"

"I know. I know it's something I need to do."

"Then, you should do it."

I think I nodded, more to myself than to her.

"I'll give you a minute." She got up and walked into the kitchen.

I didn't spend any more time thinking about it. I stepped up, whispered, "Goodbye" and tossed it all in, piece by piece, and listened to the fire crackle as it was fed.

At first, it felt so, so good.

And then, it felt so, so bad.

I didn't know how to handle the wild ride of my changing emotions, so I did what was easy and most famil-iar. I marched into the kitchen and lashed out at Gloria, "<u>You</u> encouraged me to burn those things. You're probably <u>happy</u> that I burned what I had left of Mom. You've been <u>waiting</u> to step into her shoes. I will <u>never</u> trust or talk to you again!"

Before she had a chance to reply, I turned on my heel and stormed up to my room, slamming the door behind me.

Chapter Nine

When I hung up with Alex, I knew I needed to get out of the house. Sitting there would only make me crazier. Even though it was pouring, I knew where I needed to go, so I jumped in my car and took off.

It was all I could do to not pull over to read and reread each and every one of Mom's words, but the rain was picking up, and I didn't want to be on the side of the rainy road, crying and reading as cars and trucks zipped by. I committed to waiting until I got to Blue Sky.

My phone rang and I jumped so high that I veered to the right.

I had to calm down.

I looked at my phone.

Dad.

I let the call go to voicemail.

As I pulled into the parking lot, the rain turned torrential and I realized it would be foolish to walk to the cove in this rain, with or without the letters.

I parked and turned off the ignition, putting my head back on the headrest and taking a massive breath in, holding it, and exhaling audibly through my mouth like I learned in those yoga classes Alex dragged me to.

It felt good. I let my shoulders sink lower and I took another huge breath in and out as the rain fell. I still didn't know what to do with the letters, but they didn't seem as volatile as they did a few breaths ago. I wondered if I should listen to Dad's voicemail or ignore it. Should I tell him that I had the letters or wait for him to find out on his own? When would that be? How often did he read them?

Once he knew I had them, I could never go back. I could never pretend I didn't find them, take them, read them. If I...

A loud *TAP, TAP, TAP* on the passenger-side scared the shit out of me.

My first reaction was to start the car and drive away but, before I could, the door opened.

What the FUCK...?

"Hey – I thought that was you when you pulled in, but I couldn't be sure with all this rain. Can I jump in?"

Brendan was jumping in my passenger side door before I had time to answer.

An odd mix of emotions washed over me: relief that it wasn't a serial killer; surprise that Brendan's smile was beaming at me; protective about the letters; and annoyed that he scooped them up as he got in and were now in his wet hands.

"What the FUCK, Brendan?" I grabbed the letters and put them in my lap, relieved they weren't damaged.

Brendan looked stunned that I was so short with him. I was, too.

"Shit – Sorry – What are those? I mean...shit. Should I go?"

"No, you can stay," I heard myself say as I soaked up his smile. Dammit. That smile. I forgot how he had ten versions of it. It took me a painfully long time to forget every detail of every one but, I did. And then, there they were, on full display.

And his smell. I tried to take a nonchalant whiff of him as he looked out the window at the rain, "Jesus! This came out of nowhere," he said.

"The rain or seeing me?"

"Both, I guess." He looked at me out of the corner of his eye.

I reached behind his seat to find a towel. "Bingo," I said as I pulled it forward and sniff-tested it. Not too bad. I tossed it to him. "It's from a yoga class last week, but you can use it to dry off."

"Thanks."

As he used the towel, I reached behind the seat again and placed the letters carefully back there. I saw him watch me from the corner of his eye.

"What are you doing here? I never imagined you still came out here," I said.

"I don't. Not really. Once in a while. When I need to think."

"Me too."

I wanted to feel familiar around him but his engagement sat between us, making this impromptu visit feel dirty and scandalous versus racy but comfortable.

"What do you need to think about?" we both asked at the same time.

"Nothing," we both answered simultaneously and laughed.

"You first," I encouraged.

"How long do you have?" he joked.

I smiled.

He took a deep breath. On his exhale, I barely heard him say, "I think I rushed into this engagement."

He winced, looking at me full of expectation, waiting to hear my reaction.

"Wow. I wasn't expecting that," is all I came up with, but it's all he needed to hear to let it flow.

"It seemed like a good idea a couple months ago. We were happy. I was happy." He stopped for a nanosecond and looked at me, obviously newly aware of who he was talking to.

I gave him a look that said, *It's OK. I'm OK.*

He paused. "I don't even know where to start or what to say."

I stayed quiet.

"I just wish I could press rewind. I wish I could go back to where we were a few months ago..." He kept talking, and I tried to pay attention but was distracted. And not by his signature golden tan or his green eyes that always looked darker when he was upset, like then. And not because I finally had his full attention and was giddy with excitement. I was distracted because, now that he was there, all I wanted was for him to leave so I could be alone with the letters.

"...and now it's all moving so fast and we have a date and it feels like there's no way out..."

I tuned back into what he was saying and cut him off with, "You sent out invitations, Brendan."

He looked up and into my eyes. "I know. I take it your dad got his?"

"Yup. It seems like the whole town did." I sounded bitter. Shit. I didn't want to sound bitter.

"That's what I mean. It's all anyone talks about anymore. It's all she talks about. And my mom. Even my guy friends talk about it. It's usually like, 'You dumb-ass. Why'd you do this so young?' which is worse than the idiotic and endless discussions about who will sit where and with who. I didn't even want to have a sit-down dinner. I wanted a party. That's what she wanted at first, too, but then…"

"So, why did you propose?" I cut him off again, my bitterness winning over patience.

"She thought she was pregnant."

"Oh, Brendan, I'm so sorry. She lost the baby?"

"No, she just thought she was pregnant."

"Wait, what…?"

He let out a long, tired, frustrated exhale, leaned his head back, and shut his eyes. I stared at him. Without opening his eyes, he explained, "One day, she came over really upset because she thought she was pregnant. She was late on her period or whatever. So we were freaking out. <u>She</u> was freaking out. Usually she's really laid back and super chill, but she was LOSING IT."

I felt a stab of satisfaction that Abby wasn't "super chill" <u>all</u> the time.

"So while she was losing her mind, to make her feel better, I said something like, 'It's all going to be OK. We love each other. We weren't planning on this right now, but it was in the plans, eventually, right?'

"Then she asked what I was saying and, to be honest, Elizabeth, I didn't really know what I was thinking, let alone saying. I was scared. I wanted to comfort her. The words 'Let's get married' were out of my mouth before I could really consider what that meant and, instantly, I knew it was the wrong thing to say. Pregnant or not, we're so young. But before I could take it back, she started crying happy tears and was saying, 'You're right. This is what we want. Maybe sooner than we thought but we want it.' And she went from stressed crying to happy crying and, before I could take it back, it was done.

"We went to the store and got the pregnancy test and, well, she wasn't. We both breathed huge sighs of relief, of course. And then I figured we'd go back to our regular lives. My 'We can get married' no longer a whisper in my head let alone on my tongue. Until she looked at me and said, 'Well no baby yet, which is great, of course. But it's super exciting that we'll get married!' And...and...I don't know...I just...I just couldn't say, 'Hold up. Wait. I figured we'd wait on all of it now.'"

"You could've said that, Brendan. You could have. You must want to get married on some level."

I knew I should be sympathetic. The old Elizabeth would've been. But I didn't know how I felt. It was the moment I'd been waiting for: Hearing that he wasn't sure about her. Yet, I wasn't happy. I felt sad. But for whom? Him? Me? Abby, who was excitedly planning their wedding and their lives while he complained to me about not wanting to marry her?

"You should talk to her. You can slow it all down. You owe it to yourself and to her to..."

"I don't want to slow it down. I want to call it off."

We just stared at each other. The rain was still coming down and we were still the only ones in the parking lot. I knew we shouldn't be there. I knew I wouldn't want him there with Abby, if the roles were reversed. But right then, I didn't care. I wanted to be right there. With him. Our faces were a foot apart, and I swore he was closing the gap between us.

"Do you remember the first time we came here?" he asked.

I leaned in, too. "Of course I do."

"I knew what I wanted then. Now I don't."

We locked eyes for a beat before moving slowly towards each other, both knowing that he knew <u>exactly</u> what he wanted.

Our lips touched and my breath did a quick, involuntary intake before I let it out slowly and let my shoulders fall with it. For the first time in a long time, being this close to someone felt...safe.

We were cautious at first, our lips softly finding each other, like old friends coming together after a long time apart. Our tongues started to get reacquainted and, when his right hand came to the back of my head and tangled in my hair, it felt so familiar that tears sprang to my eyes because it felt so right.

"Oh, Elizabeth...I've thought of this moment more than I should admit," he said between kissing my mouth over and over again, not even trying to get in sync with me. "I want you so bad. I think of you all the time."

He did?

All that time, I thought he never thought of me, and that he was so happy without me, and that they were so mature, and had it all figured out and...there he was, as lost and lonely as me, it seemed.

"I missed you, Elizabeth." He leaned into my ear, kissing it in the way he knew drove me nuts. I groaned and he lifted my shirt and cupped my breasts when a loud clap of thunder snapped and Brendan's car alarm started screeching. We jumped apart and, as we did, I thought of the letters in the backseat.

And the wedding invitations scattered around town.

I thought of Abby at home, flipping through bridal magazines in her pink cowboy boots.

Who knew pieces of paper could be that heavy?

I couldn't do it.

It was wrong.

"I think you should probably go, Brendan. I don't think I'm the person you need to figure this out with," I said.

"You're right. I'm so sorry." Now that the spell was broken, he couldn't even look at me as he opened the door and got out. He was about to shut the door when he asked, "Hey, was that you who drove by my house yesterday?"

I looked at him standing there in the rain, looking so lost. His cheeks still flush from our kiss, his darting eyes looking guilty and ashamed.

"It wasn't me." I lied.

"Oh. OK." He paused, wiped the rain from his brow and finally managed to make eye-contact again. "We didn't talk about why you came here to think. What's going on?"

"Nothing," I said and smiled.

"Are you sure?"

"I'm good." And I realized I was. Or, at least, I didn't need him to figure it out. "Bye, Brendan."

"Bye, Elizabeth."

I watched him scurry back to his car.

Before he pulled out of the lot, he gave me one last wave. I waved back. He had a lot to face. A lot to figure out.

I reached into the backseat.

So did I.

Chapter Ten

On a similar, stormy August day fourteen years ago, I was a sour six-year-old because our day at the jetty would be rained out.

In anticipation of kindergarten starting soon, Mom and I had planned our first picnic at Blue Sky for us and Alice. Alice was driving. Mom and I were bringing the picnic. I was beyond excited the night before and then <u>devastated</u> when we woke to torrential downpours, and the weatherman's forecast of one-hundred percent more rain, wind, and lightning. I was crushed and crying. I even refused to dance to *Three Little Birds* with Mom like we did every morning to start the day.

At first Dad was understanding, but when I wouldn't stop sobbing, he was annoyed with me and, by extension, Mom. As he left for work, I heard him scold her. "Good luck. She's being a monster, which you created by running wild with her all day. She knows NO structure. NO boundaries. NO consequences."

"She's <u>young</u>, Michael. She's supposed to be carefree. She's supposed to be happy."

"She can still be happy with those things, Eve. They're part of life. How can you not see that? Of course I want her to be happy. But she needs to learn how the real world works. She can't have a meltdown over the weather. She needs friends her own age. She needs structure."

"Why? I just don't get it. She's going to school in the fall. She'll have structure for the rest of her life. Why not let her be a kid? Why not let her run wild while she can?"

"See, you admit she's running wild!"

"Oh, for Christ's sake, Mike! Are you for real with this shit?"

"Evangeline, I don't want to keep having this conversation. If we don't get her ready for school <u>now</u>, then she'll be <u>completely</u> unprepared when she needs to go. You think you're helping her, but you're hurting her."

"<u>Completely</u> unprepared for what, exactly? It's kindergarten!"

"She won't know a soul her own age, let alone how to play with her peers all day. She needs exposure to kids her age. You need to be a part of the mom network. It will help pave the way for Elizabeth. Why can't you see that?"

"The 'mom network'? Who do you think I am, Michael? Did you think I'd <u>ever</u> want to be a part of that?"

"I should've known."

"Should've known what?"

Dad took a deep breath and let it out slowly and audibly, before saying, "I just don't understand why you refuse to sign her up for any classes, or accept the coffee and play-dates from that nice lady down the street with the daughter Elizabeth's age. Why not? It's just an afternoon. I don't know why you just won't do it."

Mom didn't respond nearly as calmly. She roared back, "Of course, you don't! You expect <u>everyone</u> to do <u>everything</u> you say, <u>when</u> you say it, <u>how</u> you want it. We're not your employees, Mike."

"Well, that's for damn sure. They actually get shit done in a day!"

"What do you want me to get done that I'm not getting done? For FUCK'S SAKE! I make sure the laundry is done, pick up the house, keep our daughter engaged and entertained, I make sure dinner is on the table. I am TRYING. None of this comes naturally to me. None of this was what I wanted..."

"STOP IT!" I screamed. Both of them whipped their heads towards me, remembering I was there. "All you do is yell at each other! All you do is fight about what's good for me!"

Mom came towards me with open arms and Dad followed her. They both wrapped around me, creating a group hug that I didn't want to end, so I just stayed silent, hoping it would bond us together like this, peaceful and happy, like we used to be.

Later, when Dad left for work, I found Mom at the kitchen table, staring straight ahead.

"What are you doing?" I asked, fearing she was about to call our neighbors to arrange a playdate. It's not that I didn't want to do that, but I had my heart set on the picnic at the jetty.

"I'm just thinking of a plan," she said.

"Oh, OK."

She could tell I was bummed. "You know, it's just that it's <u>pouring</u>, Elizabeth, and it's not supposed to let up all day and night. Your Dad will have a fit if we go in the rain and get sick. I'm sorry, but maybe this time we just do what he suggested. We can do the jetty another day, I promise," she explained.

"Alright. I understand," I said. I didn't. But I didn't want Mom to be upset, because I knew <u>she</u> wanted to go. It was Dad who didn't want us to have any fun. I'd heard him say to Mom all the time, "While you're gallivanting around, I'm living in the real world so I can pay our bills in the real world." But I didn't know what he meant. Mom worked really hard on her art. Most days, we were cruising to the art store for more supplies if she wasn't working a shift there. Sometimes she even taught classes there. And we were always going to museums and galleries to see other people's work, which she said was very important to "her process" which, I could tell, was, like, the most important thing. Plus, Dad was always saying that I should be out in the real world, and I didn't understand how us going to all these places wasn't being in the real world.

Sitting in the kitchen that rainy day made my heart feel heavy in a way it hadn't ever before. I wasn't really sad about the jetty anymore, but I didn't know how to explain why else I was sad, or that I feared, for the first time, that a "broken heart" might be a real thing. Before I had to worry about it too much more, Mom clapped her hands together and said, "I have an idea!"

"You do?"

"Come with me." She grabbed my hand and we raced upstairs.

"Go in your room and put on your art clothes."

She went into her room and I did the same. We both came out in our matching denim overalls for when we "worked together" in her studio, which pretty much meant her painting at her easel and me sitting on the couch, writing stories in these blank notebooks that she'd buy and then decorate the covers for me, per my request, depending on what I was writing about.

"Follow me," she said and we went back downstairs, through the kitchen, into the garage and over to Dad's workbench. Mom was looking at some tools and cans, and I knew to just let her do her thing.

She said, "Take this. And take this. And this," as she put a paint can in each of my hands and a paintbrush in my mouth. She did the same and somehow, managed to grab a few more things. She jerked her head in a "Follow me" gesture, because she, too, had a paintbrush in her mouth. This almost gave us the giggles. I followed her out the back door, across the lawn, and up to her studio.

When we got upstairs, I continued to follow her lead as we put everything in the middle of the room. She went over to her stereo and, after some fumbling, put on what sounded like ocean waves. She turned from the stereo with a huge smile on her face.

"My Girl, if we can't go to the jetty because of the rain, let's make the jetty in here, safe from the rain."

I looked at her, puzzled, as she started to pull all the furniture away from the walls.

"What are you doing, Mom? What do you mean? Are we making a painting together?"

"We're making more than a painting. We're going to paint the whole studio to look like Blue Sky. We'll get creative with the colors we have, but with you explaining to me what it looks like, I think we can get it close to right with what we have."

"Wait, you mean...we're going to just paint these walls? Right now?" My mind couldn't comprehend. "Do you think Dad will like this?"

"I don't know. But it's my studio. It's our workspace. Our day. Let's bring the jetty to us, and we can still have our picnic with Alice later, if we work hard. Are you in?" She put her hand in, top up, for me to put mine over.

"I'm in!" I slapped my hand on top of hers and then we repeated it.

"Let's go!" she yelled as we made our hands explode above us in the air.

And then we got started. She asked me to describe what the trip to the jetty was like in as much detail as I could remember from what I saw when I went with Alice. I gave her the rundown in two parts: First, what she asked for. Second, what the human eye couldn't see, what only our imaginations could conjure, the land of unicorns and mermaids.

For hours Mom painted and asked questions to keep me engaged. When we got to the entryway to the secret world, I explained, like Alice had done with me. *There's a wooden walkway that looks like any old wooden walkway; but it's magical because, at the end of it, if you know where and how to look at it, then a little kiosk appears where we can enter the secret password.*

I told Mom that I needed to wait for Alice to tell her the password since Alice trusted me with it and I needed to make sure she was OK with me sharing it. Mom acted solemn as she said, "I understand. And I respect that decision."

"Thanks, Mom," I said with great earnestness.

"Who knows the password?" she asked with the same seriousness.

That stumped me. "Umm... I don't know. I guess other people like us."

"Fantastic! So the brave. The bold. The beautiful dreamers."

"Exactly!" I exclaimed as I wrapped my paint-laden arms around her. Mom always got it. Always.

Our work was anything but organized that day. Anything but clean. We got paint everywhere. It was on the floor, the ceiling, the walls. And that was all intentional. But it was all over everything else in-between, including our hair and clothes.

When Alice came over that afternoon, she burst into laughter because we were completely covered in paint. But she also couldn't stop looking around and saying, "Wow."

She was right. In a few short hours, Mom managed to make her studio look like a regular beach above with a fantastical forest underneath. After Alice gave me permission to tell Mom the password – "Adventure" – we entered and spent the day.

The three of us danced around our indoor beach, drank from fancy glasses, and laughed the day away. The rain kept coming and we kept carrying on, until Alice had to leave to meet her new girlfriend. Then Mom said we needed to clean up and get dinner started. "But before we do, we have one more thing to do. We can't let the day go without doing it," and then she walked over to the stereo and put on *Three Little Birds* and we did our daily dance before trudging back across the yard in the rain, leaving rainbow streams behind us from our feet. Mom and I took a bubble bath together and then she was too tired to cook so we ordered pizza. We ate in front of the TV and when she tucked me in that night, she said as she did every night, "We're the lucky ones. We got another day together today."

"We got the <u>perfect</u> day."

"Every day with you is perfect, Elizabeth. And remember, no matter where we are, every day is perfect because the sky we look at is the same."

"Forever?"

"And ever."

"You promise?"

"I promise."

That was before I realized her promises were like silk scarves tied to tree branches on windy days; bound to come untied.

I was drifting off to sleep when I heard Dad come home and another fight ensued. I couldn't hear every word, but I got the gist.

"Not all of us can live this whimsy life, Evangeline!"

She must've said something about San Francisco, which made him yell, "Oh my FUCKING GOD, Eve. You have to let San Francisco go. I was with Gloria that whole night. Let it go."

The next morning, when Mom played our Bob Marley song, instead of dancing, I started crying.

"What's wrong, My Girl?" she said as she wrapped me in a hug.

"Well, I heard you and Dad fighting last night, and…"

"Go on, Honey. Talk to me."

"Well, if things like us dancing during the day make him so mad, then maybe we shouldn't do it anymore. I want to, but I hate it when you two fight."

"Honey, there's nothing wrong with dancing. Dad knows that deep down. He's just really stressed out about work. But I promise you, it's OK to dance. It's more than OK. It's beautiful to express yourself with movement. And art. And whatever other ways you find in life. Promise me you'll always remember that."

"I promise."

We danced every morning until she left.

After that, I didn't dance again.

* * * *

I sat there, completely still, listening to the rain hit the car's roof, trying to calm my anger towards Dad. <u>And</u> Gloria who <u>had</u> to know about the letters. I was trying to process it all. Should I tell Dad I needed to talk to him before the barbeque? Or wait until after so I would have his full attention and he couldn't duck out of the conversation? What would I even say? Was he going to deny it? How could he? Should I tell him I had the letters or just ask first if Mom ever wrote and give him a final chance to come clean?

My heart sped up. I was having trouble taking a deep breath. I needed a drink. I turned on the ignition and went through my liquor store options, debating which ones I was least likely to see anyone I knew. As I left Blue Sky and realized I likely wouldn't be back for a while, I remembered Mom's studio version of it.

I didn't go up to Mom's studio for years after she left. But one Sunday morning during my junior year, when <u>all</u>

Dad and Gloria wanted to talk about was what colleges I would apply to, and if we'd go visit the campuses, and <u>all</u> the other endless, trivial travel details they'd discuss about each potential school, they were driving me absolutely mad in every sense of the word. I had to get out of there.

I put on my running shoes and took a few laps around the neighborhood, but even that wasn't enough. When I got back they were still in the kitchen. I had to escape.

I went outside, crossed the yard and headed up the stairs, eager to be in Mom's studio, to see the jetty we created and...

Dad had wiped it clean. He painted over every bit of it. Solid white. Zero color.

I sat on the floor and wept.

* * * *

As I drove away from the jetty, I could still smell Brendan all over me. That kiss...wow. It was even better than I remembered, which said a lot because I'd been pining for a kiss from him since my last one. The bar was so high, yet, he went above it today. I guess age and experience <u>do</u> make a difference. I wonder if he'd say the same about me.

As if I needed one more thing to wonder about.

I was turning onto Main Street looking for a liquor store when a huge CLOSING SALE sign caught my attention, and then caught my heart when I realized it was in front of Sacred Art.

Before I was conscious of what I was doing, I pulled into the parking lot, jumped out of my car, and ran to the door in the rain. I got more and more soaked with every step, but turning back didn't feel like an option.

I busted into the store, soaked, and squinting from the contrast of the dark skies outside to the bright lights inside. Instantly, the smell hit me. Paper and ink and coffee and… my eyes welled up. I felt someone looking at me. Maybe the rain would mask the few tears that leaked out and make them look like raindrops.

I looked up smiling, hyper-aware of just how wet I was and that it might not be cool to be dripping in the store. What was I even doing there? I was about to turn around and walk out when I heard, "Stay right there. I'll grab some paper towels."

"Oh no, it's no worry. I'm fine. I was just about to leave," I said as my eyes found the face of the voice. The most electric blue eyes I'd ever seen were locked onto mine.

"Here you go," this blue-eyed boy said, handing me a roll of paper towels. "It's the best I can do." He didn't look more than twenty-five, but his confidence and manners made me think he was older. His hair was jet black and long in the front. He had already pushed it back two times since handing me the roll. I wanted to reach over and do it for him, just to touch him.

"You're soaked," he said and smiled.

"I know. This is just from running down the street from my car. I almost purposefully walked on the beach in the rain earlier but didn't want to get <u>this</u> wet." I gestured from my head to my toes. "I should've just gone for the beach walk."

"There's nothing like a good walk in the rain," he agreed. "There's nothing like any walk on any beach, but my favorite one, rain or shine, is about fifteen minutes from here. It's a perfect swimming beach because it's protected by a jetty, and it has a great path that winds through an almost magical forest, and there's hardly anyone there from September through May."

"I know that beach." And then it was me smiling at him.

"You do?" he asked, his surprise obvious.

"Yeah. A friend of my mom's showed it to me," I said, as he said, "An older woman from here showed it to me."

Before I could fully register his words, we both said in unison, "Alice."

"Wait! You know Alice?" I asked, dumbfounded.

"Wait. YOU know Alice? The Alice who works here? Used to work here?"

"Yeah, but I haven't seen, or even thought of her, for years. Until this week," I said, already lost in my racing thoughts. I fired questions at him. "How long have you worked here? You said, 'Alice worked here.' She doesn't anymore? Where is she?"

"Slow down," he laughed and those blue eyes sparkled. Normally, I'd be distracted by his perfect, white teeth and intimidated by his flawless, olive complexion, but I was too focused on Alice to give much thought to how heartbreakingly handsome he was.

"I've worked here for about a year and Alice worked here when I started," he continued. "I was new to the area so Alice told me some places she loved. Blue Sky is obviously one of them. How do you know her?"

"I don't. I mean, I haven't <u>known</u> her for a very long time. Alice and my mom were good friends. My mom worked here, too. They met here. They were friends here."

"Cool. Yeah, Alice is a cool lady. I was sad when she left, but she said that, after being here for twenty years, the store closing was a sign that it was time to move on, even before it sold. Can you imagine being somewhere that long? Did your mom like working here?"

"Yes."

"Why'd she'd stop working here?"

"She left. She's gone. Her and Alice used to be good friends. I think. But I don't know. I haven't talked to her in a while. My mom, I mean. And Alice." I tried to sound light and nonchalant but realized I sounded anything but with how long I'd been rambling on. *Pull it together, Elizabeth*, I scolded myself. "It's a long story."

He looked at me encouragingly, like he wanted me to continue. At least that's how I took it, so I rambled on with, "My mom was an artist and she worked here part-time, with Alice. But then my mom and dad split up and my mom left town. Or, my mom left town and then they split up." I got SUPER self-conscious. "Like I said, it's a long story."

"I'm sorry your mom left. That sucks."

"Yeah, it does." We stood there for a beat, without saying anything, until I couldn't take the silence and rushed to fill it, like I usually did. "It's OK. I just haven't thought about this all in a long time. The idea that Alice worked here as of fairly recently – that's crazy to me. But I'll let you get back to work."

"It's OK. We're about to close. I feel bad sending you back out in the rain."

"That's OK. I need to get home. It was a very, <u>very</u> long day."

I handed him back the paper towel roll but held my soaked ones in my other hand by my side. He reached for both.

"OK. Well, it was nice meeting you...?" He fished for my name.

"Elizabeth."

"Elizabeth. It's nice to meet you. I'm Josh."

"Hi, Josh."

I turned around and took a few steps. I was almost through the door when I spun back and saw that he was still watching me, smiling.

"Is there any chance you have Alice's contact information? Maybe I'm meant to reconnect with her."

"I don't." He grimaced like he wished he could help me out.

"That's OK. Well, it was nice meeting you, Josh."

I was out the door and no longer trying to outrun the rain. What was the point?

My stomach grumbled louder than the rain and I realized I hadn't eaten anything all day. I couldn't wait to be home. The last 36 hours had been...too much. When I got up yesterday morning, I figured contending with the barbeque was my biggest challenge of the week. Now there were letters, old friends...all these pieces of a puzzle I didn't realize I was dying to make.

I was so lost in my head that I didn't hear him until he was about ten steps behind me. "Elizabeth! Wait!"

I turned to see Josh jogging towards me. When he reached the awning, he gently touched my elbow, pulling me under it and protecting us from the rain. It wasn't until I was standing shoulder to shoulder with him, watching the raindrops fall heavy on the pavement that I realized I hadn't flinched. I turned to him and then he spoke, "Are you OK?"

"Yeah," I stuttered.

"Good. Elizabeth, I was thinking…I can't help you out with Alice, but I realized that the owner is in the back. He hates when we bother him when he's here at night because it's his alone time in the stockroom with his favorite radio programs and whisky, but…"

"Wait, does Mr. Owens still own Sacred Art?" Oh my God. I hadn't thought of him in longer than I'd thought of Alice, but I remembered distinctly that Mom loved that Mr. Owens and his wife had a date night every Friday in the back room, doing their inventory and slugging back a few drinks.

"Yeah, he does. He's great. Grumpy, but generally good."

"Yes! With his wife. Is she back there with him tonight?"

"I guess she died a while back. I've never met her. People say he was nicer when his wife was alive."

I felt a sadness about Mrs. Owens that seemed bigger than it should, considering I barely knew her and hadn't thought of her in a decade. But she was always kind to me. She always gave me a fruit roll-up, or trail mix, or home-made cookies. I didn't have sugar often, but Mom always let me have whatever Mrs. Owens gave me because she said it was a healthy version of sugar and given with love, which made it OK. Even so, we never told Dad because he'd say that any kind of sugar was too much sugar.

"Do you want me to ask Mr. Owens if he knows where Alice is? I know they were close. He might have a way to contact her."

"Yes! Wait, no. Yes." I shook my head again. "Wait."

He smiled and seemed to get it. "It's up to you, but to set expectations, he's pretty cranky, and we're about to close, so he might just get snippy with me and give zero info, but I can try."

I felt giddy and nervous, and I couldn't tell if it was because I might see Mr. Owens or because this handsome guy seemed to want to do nice things for me. I let my mind tumble with the possibilities for a few seconds and then, before I overthought it, said, "Yeah, let's go back and see if he knows anything."

"OK. Let's go! On the count of three we'll make a run for it. One...two...three..." We both took off sprinting down the street, back to the past and into my future.

Chapter Eleven

I heard the afternoon bells chime in the town square as I waited at the register for Josh to return from the storeroom, either with or without Mr. Owens. For the second time that day, the rain covered my true emotion because I was sweating bullets and hoping he'd think it was the rain. I considered leaving. It was kind of crazy. A guy who I had just met was about to ask an old man, who probably didn't remember my mother, let alone me, if he had contact information for a woman I hadn't thought about in years. It felt crazy, yet...comfortable.

I took slow, deep breaths to savor that familiar scent of the homemade paper that sat in irregular reams of every color and pattern imaginable. They were just as captivating as I remembered, though they felt smaller now. Mom used to pick me up and perch me on her hip so I could see the top-shelf options, but now I was as tall as the tallest shelf. Staring at the different kinds of paper still made my chest expand with the possibility of all life's stories, like it did when I was little. All the types of pens and pencils and markers. The notepads and journals and canvases. The tools of all shapes and sizes. I remember as a kid wanting to use each and every item in the shop, which felt so fiercely familiar yet foreign to the young woman standing here all those years later.

I was brought back to my surroundings when the store bell rang with a new customer.

What was happening back there with Josh and Mr. Owens? It felt like he'd been gone forever. Maybe he got in trouble for even asking and didn't want to face me. If I left then, I could spare him the moment where he had to tell me.

No sooner did I decide to flee did I hear, "Well I'll be damned! It _is_ you, Elizabeth." And there was Mr. Owens coming through the storeroom's swinging door, like he did fifteen years ago when I'd visit. His tall frame carried a little more weight than I remembered, but his deep brown eyes were as alive and warm as I remembered, and his massive, toothy grin on his long, kind face still evoked the image of a horse in my mind, so I still had to stifle a giggle like I did as a girl.

"Hello," I said, surprised I was able to get any words out.

"Let me look at you...Elizabeth! You're all grown up. You're the spitting image of your mother, that's for sure."

I am? I'd never been told that before. Nobody really remembered Mom, or at least weren't referencing her to me.

Does Dad think I look like Mom?

Had I spoken yet?

I was in a time warp.

"When Josh said that a girl named Elizabeth is here, a girl who knew Alice, and whose own mother used to work here, I thought, *She finally came for a visit. I knew she would.* If only Mrs. Owens was here. Josh told me he told you that she passed on. God rest her soul." He crossed himself. I forgot how often he did that in a day. Mom said it was the only thing she didn't trust about him, but only because she didn't trust organized religion.

"What brings you here? Oh no, is it your mother? Do you have bad news? Is that why you need to reach Alice?"

"No, I don't have bad news. I mean...I don't know why I'm here. It was a whim when I saw the CLOSING sign. And then Josh and I chatted and he mentioned Alice, who I've also lost touch with, and next thing I know, here you are." I smiled weakly. I wanted to give him a megawatt smile, but I was exhausted, and it was confusing, and I kind of wished I could press rewind and not come inside.

"Honey, I'd love to put you and Alice in touch. We actually talked about you often, especially after she'd have a phone date with your mom once she left town."

My eyes pricked with tears. "Wait, what?" My voice betrayed me and sounded every bit of the emotion that ripped through my gut. "They talked once Mom left?"

"Oh, sure, honey." And then he put it all together. "Why, did you not...?"

"No. I never heard from her again."

"Oh, dear. That doesn't sound like Eve. Not at all. Oh dear."

I wanted to run. I wanted to escape the moment.

But it felt like I needed to stand there, like something important and impactful was coming my way if I could just stand there, stay there, find my voice to ask some questions.

"I'm sorry about your wife, Mr. Owens. I always liked Mrs. Owens. She was kind to me," I said, suddenly nostalgic and longing for someone I hadn't seen in fifteen years.

I could still picture her graying blonde hair. She reminded me of a walking mermaid because she was the tallest woman I knew and it seemed like that much length should have a tail on the end. And her curly hair was wild like the waves and she was always trying to tame it with pencils that she'd pull out of her messy bun when needed. But what I remember most clearly was the morning her granddaughters came to visit her while I was there, waiting for Mom to get off work.

When the three little girls came running in, I felt protective of the store and of Mrs. Owens. Who were these girls who ran in like they owned it and then spring-boarded onto Mrs. Owens? Wherever they landed, she managed to catch and hold them all. I was staring when Mrs. Owens said, "Come meet my granddaughters, Elizabeth. Mable is about your age."

I didn't really want to know these girls, who seemed important to Mrs. Owens, but I went over to meet them. And we did end up having fun for a little while before Mom got off work. But, as much fun as it was, I remembered coveting their unlimited access to the store and Mrs. Owens.

As soon as Mom and I left the store to walk home, I had a million questions.

"Mom, since both my grandmothers are gone, can we ask Mrs. Owens to be my new grandmother?

"Oh, Sweetheart – That's lovely, but it doesn't work that way."

"Then how does it work? And where did my grandmothers go?"

"We've talked about this before. But…let's see, OK. Dad's mom – her name was Phyllis – died in a car accident, with his father, Jasper. He was…is…your grand<u>father</u>."

"They died?"

"Yes. You knew that, Honey. A long time ago. I never met them. This happened before I met Dad."

"Did Dad know them?"

"He did. He was twelve when they died."

"Oh no. Poor Dad. What did he do when he didn't have parents anymore?" The thought terrified me, which Mom read on my face, so she quickly added, "That's when he moved in with Uncle Will and his family. You know all of them. Dad loves them. It all ended up OK."

I was silent for a little while, trying to process what this meant. I was trying not to be afraid, or sad, because it didn't seem like Mom was, so maybe it wasn't scary or sad, even if that's how it felt. When we were almost home, I turned to Mom. "Wait. We didn't talk about your mother. Where is she?"

"She's gone."

"Gone?"

"Yes, gone. I don't know her."

"Is she dead? Like Grandmother Phyllis?"

"She might be. She might as well be. I'm not sure."

I started to panic. This could happen? Moms could just disappear?

"Sweetheart, I can see your worried face. It's all OK. I shouldn't have said it like that. It's more like...me and my mother, your Grandmother Annabelle, or Anna, we just didn't...it was just better to...You know what, this is a conversation for another time. I'm tired. You're tired. Let's go in, order pizza and a movie, and call it a week. Dad will be home soon. How does that sound?"

But where was this Grandmother Anna? I knew I'd have to wait until I got to Heaven to meet Grandmother Phyllis, but maybe I'd meet this Grandmother Anna some-day. Maybe someday I could catapult myself towards her, and she'd catch me no matter where I landed, and we'd laugh and have fun together. I think I'd like that.

* * * *

"Olive loved your mother, Elizabeth. We both did. Oh dear… are you OK?" Mr. Owens mistook my spacing out about my long-lost grandmothers as being upset, but before I could explain, he said, "Let's change the subject. I want to hear more about you. Are you still an artist yourself?"

"An artist? No, I was never an art…"

"Sure you were! You wrote the loveliest, most capti-vating short stories."

Mr. Owens rummaged around in a drawer and then, from the very back, pulled something out. "I knew I still had it in here! Look! This is the one you wrote about Sacred Art. I saved it all these years because, well, we just loved it. And, look, that's your Mom's work on the front."

He handed me the palm-sized notebook and the image on the cover nearly knocked me off my feet. It was a cartoon-like, but realistic, version of the front of Sacred Art and there, standing in the window, with a book in one hand and a pencil in the other, is young me, looking out at the world on a bright, sunny day. I remembered how often she used to paint me. I wondered where all Mom's art went. Did she take it with her? Did Dad toss it? So many new questions. New options. New angles.

I couldn't tell if my heart was racing in excitement or in warning. Either way, I couldn't let this moment go. If I didn't ask then, when would I? I feared the answer, but I needed to know.

"Mr. Owens, it would be great to reconnect with Alice, too, since this has been so nice, seeing you after all these years. Well, <u>really</u> seeing you, and talking to you." I looked down, suddenly wishing I hadn't just let them slip away all those years ago. I'd pass both Owens in the grocery store, or on the street, or wherever, through the years. When Mom first left, we always waved and were warm towards one another, but I could tell that Dad wanted nothing to do with them, so it never went beyond a distant wave. By the time I was out and about in Wellbury, bumping into them on my own from time to time, it had been so many years that I forgot our connection from those early years.

Mr. Owens smiled big. "We always loved watching you from a distance, us three here at the shop. Olive and

Alice and I would update each other if we saw you. I'm sure Alice passed that along to your mother, too. I didn't realize you were still estranged. I figured by now, it would have worked itself out. But here you are, after all these years, and right before we close for good. I'm so happy to see you. You and your mother were a huge part of this store. And your mom's belief that art could change lives permeated this place long after she left."

"So you probably haven't spoken to her since then, right? Since she left?"

There it was. The question I needed to ask but didn't really want the answer to: When had Mom last been in touch with him? And what about Alice? Recently? Like, she was reachable, and had been for all those years, but just not to me?

My head spun, but I didn't want Mr. Owens to know, nor Josh, who had been quietly taking it all in as he went about the cleanup process, one that I recognized so clearly from closing up with Mom that I probably could've jumped in to help.

Mr. Owens looked troubled as he started to answer. "Well, no dear, Alice hasn't worked here for a while now – but she was in touch with your mother until she left. At least I think she was."

No matter how much I tried to keep my outward appearance the same, my face must've fallen because he followed it up with, "But I might be wrong, Elizabeth. Oh, dear, I'm not sure."

My heart went out to him. I put on my best smile. "Mr. Owens, it's all good. Really. This has all been an unexpected walk down Memory Lane, hasn't it?"

I wanted to ask for Alice's contact information, but I mean, did I really want it? What would I do with it? As recently as a few years ago, she was in touch with Mom. Hell, she might <u>still</u> be in touch with her. That meant, throughout high school, when I was running into Alice here and there, she was in touch with Mom. Like, she could call her. At least it sounded like she could. I didn't even know how to start wrapping my head around that.

I wanted to get out of there before I got more upset and embarrassed myself. I was about to say I had to get going when Mr. Owens said, "Listen, dear, I'm due to call Alice for a catch up. How about if I try her now, and tell her you're here, and see if she wants to say, 'Hello' or ask if I can give you her number?"

My heart was in my throat. "Oh, I don't know about that...that's...that's not necessary..."

"You should do it," Josh piped up from the back of the store. "Just do it." His electric blue eyes were speaking to my soul.

"OK, Mr. Owens. Let's try it. That'd be great. But tell her no pressure or anything," I said self-consciously, imagining all the ways this could go wrong and lead to more disappointment.

"Oh good! Here we go! Some unexpected excitement for the night." He reached under the counter and pulled out an address book that looked as old as he was. I realized he was doing it right there, right then, right in front of me. I tried to act cool, but I wanted to run, either outside the store, or even quicker, to the corner of the store to rock back and forth.

He took a while to find the number and then dialed from the landline. The whole thing would've been sweet, endearing, and even a little comical if I wasn't about to have a panic attack.

Once the number was dialed, he covered the phone receiver and said, "She'll be surprised to hear from me."

I smiled encouragingly. At least I hoped that's what I was conveying. I felt so upside-down that I couldn't be sure.

After about five more seconds that felt more like five years, he covered the phone again and said, "I'm getting her answering machine." And then he said in a bright, booming voice into the phone, "Good afternoon, Alice! Mr. Owens here. I have a surprise for you. You won't believe it. Call me when you get a chance." Then he gave his phone number three times before hanging up.

"Alice loves a good adventure. She'll be dying to know my surprise and I expect to hear from her soon."

My heart started to slow, knowing the moment was over. I was equally happy and heartbroken.

And then, just when it felt back to normal, he said, "You know, dear, I feel badly about saying that Alice and your mother kept up until Alice left. As I was waiting for her to answer, I started to think about it and realized that, actually, I remember Alice saying that she hadn't heard from your mother in a while. It seems they lost touch, too."

I didn't know how to feel about that. In some ways, I felt better that Mom lost touch with Alice, too, but in other ways, I wished they were in touch so Alice might know how to find her.

I was about to leave, yet again, when Mr. Owens said, "I think that's right, now that I do think about it. I'm sorry for the confusion, dear. My mind isn't what it used to be."

"That's quite alright, Mr. O." We both smiled at the nickname I hadn't uttered in fifteen years. "I'm just happy to see you, and that you tried Alice for me."

"Oh good, dear. I know she'll be delighted to hear you're looking for her. I am sure of it. Swing in tomorrow. It's our final day. And I'm sure she'll call back so I should have an update for you by then."

I was about to suggest he take my number and give it to her, but I wanted another reason to come back and see him. And, I'd be lying if I said I didn't want to see Josh, too.

"Sounds like a plan, Mr. Owens. I'll do that."

"Lovely. We can do some more catching up. It is such a pleasure to see you again. Wow, just look at you. I know Evangeline would be proud."

I wondered what emotion she'd have about me, but I didn't say it. Instead, I smiled brightly. "I'll see you again soon, Mr. Owens. And, Josh, thanks for your help."

"My pleasure." He started walking with me to the door which now had sunlight beaming through the glass plate, causing us to squint at each other. God, it's crazy how quickly things can change.

"I hope I'm here when you come back tomorrow because I'm leaving Wellbury now that the store is closing. I'm headed to Boston."

"You are?"

"Yeah, just when I'm meeting you."

"Well, I go to school in Boston."

"What? Where? Law school? Masters?"

"I'm in college." I winced so he knew that I knew that it wasn't ideal.

"SHUT UP!"

"No, I am. Really."

"Wait...really?"

"Yeah." I tried to give my most mature, most seductive smile.

"Are you at least a senior?"

"A sophomore."

He made an explosion sound and held his heart like I just shot him.

"Why...how old are you?"

"Twenty-five."

Shyly, I ventured forward with, "That's not too big of a leap."

"It is if you're not twenty-one. My personal code dictates that I can't date anyone too young to have a legal drink with me at dinner, if they choose to."

I tried to ignore the word "date" and keep it cool when I said, "Not twenty-one yet."

"Damn. When is your birthday?"

"February 27. Just a few months."

"Well, Mr. Owens said you're a writer, so until then, why don't you send me some of your stuff and we'll keep in touch like that."

"Oh, I'm not a...I don't have anything written."

"Then, write me something," he smiled. Was this even happening? I felt like I was in one of those cheesy movies where the girl is all, *Pinch me, this can't be real.*

"OK. Sure. Maybe." *Pull it together.*

He smiled, "Well, I hope you do – I'd love to read it. But, either way, I'll look forward to seeing you again tomorrow. And, I have to admit, Elizabeth, my curiosity is piqued."

So was mine when I realized his smile rivaled his eyes for best feature.

"Oh yeah? About what?"

"All of it," he smiled.

Chapter Twelve

"What the FUCK are you <u>thinking</u>, Evangeline?" is what stopped me, Mom, and Alice dead in our tracks, all those years ago up in Mom's studio. We were up there celebrating an art workshop that Mom and Alice had done at the store that morning. They were done early and giddy with success. One moment, us three were grooving to some reggae, and the next, Dad was charging up the stairs and into the open door, stopping us cold like we were playing a game of freeze tag with Dad's angry voice as the freeze trigger.

"Mike, what are you doing home?" Mom broke into a huge smile, as if it wasn't clear the mood that Dad was already in. "We weren't expecting you until dinner, were we Elizabeth?" she asked, gesturing to me, as if to remind him that I was in the room.

"I know she's here, Evangeline. That's why I'm upset. You think it's OK to act this wild in front of her, in the middle of the day nonetheless?"

"Mike, your yelling is the only wild thing happening right now," Alice interjected.

"Shut up, Alice. Better yet, isn't it time to go home to your own family? Oh wait, you don't have one, so you don't know what you're talking about."

"Watch yourself, Mike. And don't talk to me like that," Alice said coolly.

"OK. This is getting to be a bit much. Alice, let's call it a day," Mom said as she crossed the room to turn the stereo down.

Alice looked bewildered. "What the...? This isn't right, Eve. You can't let this fly."

Mom stopped on her way to the stereo and gently placed her hands on Alice's shoulders. "It's OK, Alice."

"But it's not."

"I know, but just the same, let's call it a day," Mom said in a much lower voice and nodded my way.

"OK, you two lovebirds. Wrap it up," Dad snarled.

"Enough, Mike! Now you're just being ridiculous," Mom snapped.

"Oooh...looks like I got under your skin."

"Stop it, Mike. STOP. IT."

"Whatever, Eve. Just ask her to leave, please."

"No need. No need," Alice said as she shook her head. She looked over to where I was still frozen and gave me a big smile and a little salute, like she did every time she said goodbye.

I saluted back, but made it smaller than usual because I worried Dad would be mad.

Mom had regained her composure and went back to acting as if nothing was amiss as Alice gathered her things and said, "Call me if you need me."

Mom said, "Oh, we're fine. We'll have a delicious dinner and a quiet night I'm sure."

Alice did the same, tiny shake of her head as if she still couldn't believe what was happening, and she left.

I hadn't noticed Mom smoking until he walked over to her and grabbed the cigarette. "Weed and white wine at 3:30 p.m., Evangeline? With your daughter here? Dancing with your friends like you're at a fucking club?"

"I had fun, Dad."

He turned towards me and I felt fear for the first time. It wasn't that I was afraid of him, but I was afraid of a world where people could change that instantly and drastically with zero warning. His enraged face only lasted an instant and then he smiled. "Honey, I'm sorry I yelled. Let's go to the house and let Mom clean this up."

I wanted to stay to help Mom like I always did, but I could tell that it would be best if I just went with him, so I did.

Mom stayed to clean up. It wasn't that messy, but it took her so long that I heard Dad go back up to the studio. I followed and crouched at the bottom of the stairs to listen.

"When I said, 'Stay to clean it up' I didn't mean stay until you drink and smoke your entire stash. What the FUCK have you been doing up here?"

"I've been doing what you said, Boss. I've been cleaning up from my wild Friday afternoon up here."

"It's fucking Thursday," Dad said with so much force his mouth might as well have been a gun and his words bullets.

"That's what I meant. Jesus!"

"No, you didn't. You actually thought it was Friday, didn't you?"

"Who fucking cares, Mike?"

"I don't know anyone who <u>doesn't</u> care what day it is, Eve." On that last part, his voice started to soften. He sounded more defeated than mad, but Mom was just getting started.

"Then, yet again, it's clear we come from two different worlds, Mike. And I'm trying to find ways – I really want to find ways – to live in your world, to make you happy, to give you the life you want. But what about the life I want? The life I deserve?" Mom's voice got louder in bursts as she went around shutting the windows, which signaled they were coming down soon. I high-tailed it back to the house and jumped on the couch like I'd been there all along, hoping my breathing could calm by the time they followed.

A minute later, they walked in together, which made me hopeful for a second, but then Dad went to his office and Mom went to shower. I sat on the couch, staying present but out of the way, wondering what would happen next.

It was a silent dinner. Halfway through I said, "If we're not going to talk tonight, can we have dinner in front of the TV as a treat?"

Mom said, "Yes" as Dad said, "No."

We all stayed at the table. Eating in silence.

Chapter Thirteen

To get ready for the barbeque, I alternated between super-hot and freezing-cold water for ten cycles. Alex swore by it as a hangover cure, if you can't get into the ocean.

Once I was out of the shower, I started to sweat – literally sweat – as I stood in front of my closet and thought about what I'd wear. Usually I planned my outfit weeks in advance, but I hadn't even thought of it. I started to imagine Rob's friends, and wondered who knew what, and how they might or not be judging me and everything about me. And then I thought about walking in and confronting Dad and…it all felt like too much. What I was wearing should've been a small thing, but it started to feel like an insurmountable decision.

I started to unravel just as I heard *DING* on my phone. It was a text from Ruth: *I'm popping over – Change of plans for me – I hope it's OK.*

A change of plans? From Ruth? I thought I'd have Ruth as support when I confronted Dad and Gloria, but now I'd have to do it alone. Before I could fully process it, I heard a knock at the door and then Ruth's voice, "Hey, Elizabeth – You here?" And the next thing I knew, Ruth was bounding up the stairs.

"What's up?" I asked as she busted into my room.

"I hope you're not mad, but...I'm not gonna make the barbeque after all. I just found out there's a <u>big</u> party that all my friends are going back to school early for, and I <u>really</u> want to go. You don't care, do you?"

"Whatever."

"Shit. I'm sorry, Elizabeth. I really didn't think you'd mind. Shit. Are you about to cry? Oh no, Elizabeth...I'll bail on the party and stay."

I was trying to control the shaking in my voice because I was afraid that, if I gave into it, I'd start a full-body shake. And I couldn't do that. But how could I confront Dad and Gloria all alone? How could I march into the barbeque and demand answers? How could I walk into the barbeque at all?

I was about to give into the shakes and the truth, and share all of it with Ruth, my oldest and dearest friend. I could tell her about Rob. About Mom's letters. About kissing Brendan. About..." It's just...I don't know what to wear," is what came out instead.

"OK...? Well...then let's go figure it out," she said like she knew there was so much more to it, but was rolling with it. She walked into my closet and started flipping hangers. "Do you have anything in your suitcase that you could wear? What did you wear all summer?"

I pulled out my go-to black capri pants and a few t-shirts I had rocked all summer.

"These could work. Simple. Classic. Not trying too hard. What do you have for jewelry?"

And then the past year slipped away and we were back in our routine, chatting and getting ready. We slipped into being funny and fun together, and I realized just how much I missed Ruth. And just how much <u>she</u> had changed. I'd been so focused on how I'd changed, that I hadn't considered how she had, too.

"Hey, I meant to ask, did you go on another date with that dude, what was his name?"

"Fred. Ugh, no." She rolled her eyes and smiled.

"Let me guess, he chews with his mouth open?"

"No, gross. I wouldn't have gone out with him at all if he did that," which made us both laugh because it was true.

"So what was wrong with him? It sounded like you were into it."

"I was, but he got on my nerves after a while. He was just...too much."

"Like he was too…what? Opinionated? Loud?" I tried to think of other traits she hated.

"No, it was more physical," she blushed.

"Well, now you have to give me the scoop," I urged her on.

"He always wanted to have sex in public places."

"Does that mean you did it at least once?"

She laughed.

"Ruth, tell me!"

"Yes, alright! At first, I was like, OK, it's not really my thing, but he's excited about it, so I'll get excited about it. I liked him that much. But, then it's, like, all he wanted to do was talk about places we could do it, and plan it out, and actually do it."

"Wow. I didn't see that coming," I smiled.

"I know. Who knew I had it in me?"

"So…?"

"So what?"

"So where did you do it? Come on, tell me!" I taunted her and felt myself smiling like I hadn't smiled in a long time.

"In his car, in the mall parking lot, at like, 8 p.m.!" she managed to squeak out as her cheeks got so red that they almost faded her freckles.

"No shit! Who are you and what did you do with my best friend?"

"I could say the same to you."

"Touché."

"Sit down. Let me do your eye makeup," she said and patted the bed next to her as I grabbed my makeup case.

We sat, inches apart, looking into each other eyes, and we smiled.

"Close your eyes," she instructed and got started on my eye shadow as she kept talking. "Now that I'm having more fun, you know, drinking and dancing and making fun more of a priority, I kind of wish that in high school we had been a little more..."

"Fun?" I filled in the blank with a chuckle.

"We were fun!" she said with mock offense. "Open your eyes and look up," she said, looking for the eye-liner.

"I know we were," I said, and gently smiled as I looked up and appreciated the moment's stillness.

"I was going to say 'adventurous' but, sure, 'fun' works too," Ruth kept talking once she started applying.

"Back then I wanted to, but it never seemed like you wanted to so I didn't push it," I admitted.

"I didn't back then. And I've wondered about that this year. Like...why was I so against it?"

I thought she was saying it rhetorically and wasn't going to answer it for herself, but then she kept talking. "I think...I don't know...it's kind of embarrassing to admit, but I think that, on some level, I didn't want to go to parties in high school, or branch out too far in any direction, because I was afraid of losing you."

"What?"

"To the cooler group. The prettier girls."

"What?! Ruth! You would've <u>never</u> lost me. You were all I had. You were what got me through when Mom left."

"Yeah, and I guess, on some level, I wanted to keep it that way."

We both sat there in silence while she finished my eye makeup. When she was done, she said, "Now, let's see."

I stood up and took a step away from her. "Do I look OK?"

"You look beautiful. You always look beautiful, Elizabeth."

I had so much I wanted to say in return. I wanted to tell her that I really missed her. That she was the one who saved me when Mom left. That without her I would have crumbled. That after last summer I constantly wished that we could be 15 again and cuddled up watching movies on Friday nights; and how I was so scared of being alone and getting older and having to face this BBQ alone. I wanted to tell her I will always love her for being the friend I needed when everything was lost...But instead, I said nothing. And before I could find the words I was looking for, she clapped her hands together and said, "My work here is done. I should hit the road."

And, just like that, the moment was over.

I was sad to see her go. I wished we had a sleepover planned so we could stay up long into the night, talking everything out until we solved all our problems, like we used to. I wanted to make promises to stay in better touch, to see each other again soon.

But, instead, I just watched her leave.

Chapter Fourteen

Dad started doing annual company parties after Gloria arrived. Mom was always encouraging some kind of a holiday party, or <u>something</u> like that, so Dad's growing team could have some fun together, but he always disagreed and insisted the crew would rather get cash bonuses for the money he'd spend on a party. Then, Gloria came along and said annual parties were good for teamwork, and company loyalty, and retention, and then Dad was on board. I'm not sure if he had changed, or if Gloria just spoke his language better than Mom did; but once it was Gloria's idea and based on business language instead of emotional language, Dad started doing parties.

He always had pool parties at rotating hotels so he could patronize his increasing list of hotel clients. But, actually, there was never anybody actually barbequing. It was more like passed appetizers and cocktails. Some people swam. Sometimes. But not really. And kids weren't invited, which is why Dad let me invite Ruth. So, it's funny that "barbeque" held up because it never really was one.

Regardless of what it had been in the past, this year, given the fifteenth anniversary, Gloria convinced Dad that change was good, so the event took on a "Game Night" theme at a new place we'd never held it before. I was worried about finding it when the hotel's flashing neon sign guided me into the parking lot. When I saw Dad's logo superimposed on the side of the building in a Vegas-style script, I wondered if tonight really was the right time to confront Dad and Gloria. But that thought was fleeting as an image of them huddled together, plotting to keep the letters from me flooded my mind.

Fuck them.

As I pulled into a spot, I resolved to confront them. Then and there. I wouldn't do it in front of everyone, but I couldn't go through the entire event and pretend to be OK with them. I'd confront them and then leave. I was sure it would be a long night once Dad got home later and we really battled it out, but I couldn't wait until then to wage the war.

Then, tomorrow, I'd head back to school, stopping to see Mr. O and Josh on the way.

As I walked into the hotel lobby, I looked around for people I knew. People who Rob knew. People who might've noticed me getting sloshed last year, or us leaving the parking lot together, or whatever. But there were a ton of extra people there. That was another change this year: Everyone could bring a plus-one. Again, something I now remembered Gloria mentioning in recent months but ignored until now.

As my eyes adjusted from the lobby to the ballroom and I took a look around, I was impressed with Gloria before I remembered I was pissed at Gloria – The place really did look like a Vegas casino.

I spotted Gloria and walked towards her. On my way, I heard, "Hey, Elizabeth," and instantly broke out in a cold sweat. I knew that voice. It was Rob's buddy. I couldn't remember his name, but I remembered his voice. It was as high-pitched and screechy as you could get while still sounding like a dude. I turned to see him and a few other faces that looked vaguely familiar, but with all the plus-ones mixed in, and because it was kind of dark, it was hard to see who was there.

I gave a quick "hello" and kept moving. I reminded myself that they hadn't done anything wrong except be friends with an asshole. And, even though I could've sworn they were staring and snickering, I had no reason to be rude to Dad's crew. But I didn't have to stop. I kept my eyes focused on Gloria and kept walking when I heard a loud voice booming over the sound system. "Umm...Hello, Everyone!

Can I please have everyone's attention…?" It was Scott, Dad's Right-Hand Man.

At that point, Dad walked up to Gloria and they turned to Scott. I stayed where I was.

"Alright, everyone, settle down, because I'm scared shitless of being up here on this microphone so if I don't do this soon, I might just leave – and that's not the 'mic drop' moment I was looking for," Scott said as everyone cheered, including Dad.

"I'm sure our fearless leader will get up here and make a speech at some point, like he always does, where he makes us feel great about the work we've done, and thanks us and makes us feel appreciated."

"Jeez, no pressure!" Dad heckled Scott from the crowd.

Scott continued, "But before he does, we wanted to get up here and sing <u>his</u> praises. If you ask around, nine out of ten people say Mike is the best boss they've ever had."

Scott waited a beat and then added, "And, Mike, find me later and I'll tell you who the one out of ten is."

Everyone laughed. I had to hand it to him, he was killing it.

"As a team, we felt we couldn't let this big anniversary go by without saying our own 'Thank you' to Mike.

"Mike, you lead by example in how to show up, for yourself, and for your team, each and every day. Perfectly on time. Never late."

Again, everyone laughed.

"You make a plan, and you stick to it, which is admirable or annoying, depending on how hungover the crew is." Scott's goofy smile reminded me that Dad always said it was disarming and helpful in business. He obviously had a fan club by all the hoots and hollers he was getting from the crowd. I tried to lighten up. Everyone was having a good time. I tried to let my guard down, despite this nagging feeling I had that it was about to go sideways for me, though I wasn't sure how. But I just knew. And then, there it was...

"Without further ado, let's roll it," Scott said, taking a seat and all of a sudden, we were looking at a huge video screen that I hadn't noticed was there until then. Up first on the video was Jane who explained that, to prove that Dad's the best boss, she asked employees past and present to share one thing they love about him, or an anniversary wish, or whatever.

I tried to breathe regularly...in and out. I tried to stay calm. But as face after face appeared on the screen, from all Dad's years in business, in videos from all over the country, even London in one case, I tried to go to another place mentally. I knew what was coming.

I thought of leaving. I could text Dad and Gloria to say, "I don't feel well all of a sudden," and then slip out unnoticed. I was about to when a gigantic version of Rob's face came on the screen.

I couldn't look.

"Hey, everyone – It's Rob coming at you from East Texas. I'm so bummed I'm not there to..."

I couldn't listen.

I jumped up and ran for the exit. A graceful, nonchalant departure was scrapped as I sprinted out of the ballroom, weaving through endless slot machines and blackjack tables as I tried to tune-out the sound of his voice and his praise of Dad. All I could think of was getting out of that room as quickly as possible.

I tried to keep breathing calmly, but it was impossible as I ran across the hallway to the bathroom and into the handicap stall. I latched the lock, leaned against the wall, and started to hyperventilate.

A few seconds later, I heard, "Elizabeth?"

I couldn't speak. I hoped she'd just go away.

"Which one are you in?"

I gasped for air, but the harder I tried, the harder it was to get any.

I couldn't catch my breath.

I couldn't get a full breath of air.

I started shaking.

"That's it. I'm coming in." And then Gloria was shimmying on her back, under the door and into the stall.

I was so stunned that I stopped thinking about breathing and actually caught my breath.

When she was all the way in, she popped up and faced me.

"I know, Elizabeth."

"Know what?"

She looked at me with love and strength in her eyes. "Elizabeth, I know."

"You don't know..."

"I do, Elizabeth. I do. I know about Rob."

I looked into her eyes, and when I saw her pain and concern beyond her love and strength, I was convinced that, yes, somehow, she knew. "But how? What?" I stammered.

She just stood there, holding my gaze until, finally, she spoke. "I know we have so much to talk about, but right now I'm trying hard not to _freak out_ about how I got into this stall. I might throw up."

And then, when I least expected it, I laughed from the bottom of my belly, until it naturally faded away, and Gloria said, "Let's get out of here. I need a shower. And we can talk, about whatever you want to share."

"How do you know...what do you know...?" Then, with utter horror, I asked, "Does Dad know, too?"

"No. Just me."

"But how?"

Chapter Fifteen

The first time I got my period, it was at school on the only day that both Ruth and Mrs. Miller were home sick. Since Mom Miller was a teacher, we had a plan that if one of us ever got it for the first time at school, we'd go to her and say, "My friend came unexpectedly," so she'd know what happened.

But she wasn't there that rainy, cold day in seventh grade when I went to the bathroom to try to dry off, thinking the seat of my pants felt wet from the rain. When I dropped my pants and saw the blood, I felt faint and FREAKED OUT. For all the times I wondered when I'd get it, it took me by such surprise that I thought, *I'm dying* before I thought, *I got my period.*

When I realized I wasn't dying <u>or</u> soaked down to my skivvies, and that my period arrived, I didn't feel relieved; I felt alone.

I wanted Mom.

But, as usual, I'd have to settle for Dad.

I huddled in the stall and pulled out my "For Emergencies Only" phone because, surely, this counted as one.

Dad picked up on the first ring. "Honey, what's wrong?"

I started crying. Not really because I got my period but, because, well, I don't know really. I guess because I felt alone. And a little scared.

"Honey, talk to me. Where are you? What's wrong?"

I realized I was causing Dad to panic so I just blurted out, "I got my period and Mrs. Miller isn't here and I don't know what to do."

"Oh, is that all? Thank God."

"Dad! What do you mean, 'Is that all?' This is a VERY BIG deal."

"I know, Honey, I know. You just scared me with the emergency call and the tears. But, let's think."

"There's nothing to think about, Dad. Come get me RIGHT NOW. Please."

"Honey, listen, I wish I could, but I'm away, pricing a job. I'm gonna be awhile. You'll have to call Gloria."

"Dad! No way! She'll try to...I don't know...she'll try to make this a bigger deal than it is to bond with me or whatever."

"No, she won't. Just calm down. It's all OK. And it's not a big deal to call Gloria. She won't make a big deal out of it. Just call her."

I walked to the nurse's office and told her that I felt really sick and needed to go home, but that my Dad was away for the day on business, so could she call the next person on the list, who I knew was Gloria. The nurse called her and she was there within fifteen minutes.

As soon as I got in the car, I started crying and told her what happened.

"Oh, Elizabeth, how wonderful."

"Wonderful? WONDERFUL?!"

"Yes, wonderful." She smiled softly at me and tilted her head. "It's wonderful, because it means that you're a woman now. It's a wonderful, beautiful thing."

"Gross."

She laughed. "Let's go inside. You can jump in my tub, have some tea, and relax for a bit. Then you can change into some of my PJs and we'll watch TV and have a snack. Sometimes, that's what getting your period calls for."

"I can live with that."

She laughed, seemingly enjoying this whole thing. I remember thinking simultaneously that I wished she had her own daughter, but was also glad she didn't.

It never seemed odd that she never had kids because, well, Mom didn't want me after all. And the Millers only had Ruth. Alice didn't have kids. I never thought to question why Gloria didn't. She didn't seem like she <u>needed</u> a kid, I guess. She always seemed to be her own entity. Part of our family, and her own family, but always on her own terms.

* * * *

Then it was seven years later and I was looking at the clock, wondering if the barbeque was still raging.

After Gloria lied to Dad and said I got my period unexpectedly we headed out. He was having too much fun to realize I had just used that excuse. That, or he had no idea how it really worked. Regardless, Gloria said it was all good. And then there we were, sitting on opposite ends of her couch, under her coziest and craziest-looking blanket.

"Tonight, I'm your friend," Gloria said. "Not your Dad's best friend. You have my confidence. I won't share anything you share with me. You can trust me."

I nodded.

"And we don't have to talk about anything you don't want to talk about, Elizabeth. This is all about you. Whatever you need."

I nodded. It wasn't that I didn't want to talk. It's just that I didn't know what to say. I still didn't know what she knew. Or thought she knew.

"What do you know?" I barely recognized my own, strangled voice, and wondered if I actually said it out loud until I could see the words racing in her mind. I could see concern for me careening across her face. "I <u>think</u> I know that Rob took advantage of you after last year's barbeque. I think he sexually assaulted you."

I nodded.

Gloria's face cracked for a second as she fought back tears and rage, but she kept her composure, and instead just nodded once back to me. We held eye contact for a few seconds and then she stood up, walked into the kitchen, grabbed a bottle of tequila and two coffee mugs, and stood in front of me. She lifted them up between us.

I nodded.

She poured two shots, handed me one, and said, "To you."

After we took the shot and laughed at each other's unavoidable I-just-did-a-shot-of-tequila grimace, we settled back into silence for a bit. The tequila had warmed my throat, my stomach. Loosened my shoulders. I took a deep inhale and exhaled.

It was finally dark outside. How was it only 8 p.m.? How much more did I have in me tonight?

Gloria sensed that I was ready to talk. "Why don't we start with what I know?"

"OK," I said, in that same, strangled-but-growing-stronger-voice that kept coming from somewhere inside.

"You know, I've had a year to think about what I'd say to you when this moment came.

"I waited and wondered when it would come. Every time you called me, I thought, *This could be it. This could be when she tells me.* But you never brought it up, so I'd have more time to think about what I'd say when you finally did. And, now that we're here, I feel speechless. Now that I'm looking at your beautiful, strong, resilient face..." A single tear rolled down her cheek.

"It's OK, Gloria."

"No, it's not. And that's OK." She took a deep, centering breath and then told me what she knew. "Last year, I had my eye on you and Rob at the party. I could tell you were flirting. I could see that it was heading somewhere. I liked Rob well enough, but that didn't mean I liked him for you.

"I saw you two leave separately and figured I had it wrong. Until the next day, when I saw you." Gloria tucked her legs underneath her and rolled her shoulders back. I could see her mind working overtime to find the right words.

"I could tell instantly that something happened. I assumed it was Rob. I blamed myself for not doing more to stop you two from flirting...from leaving together. For choosing to believe that you weren't leaving together.

"I asked you if everything was OK and you said 'fine' in a way that said you were anything but fine, but didn't want to talk.

"I kept asking and asking, and you said nothing was wrong and that you were 'just stressed about school.' And, well, that could've been, so I hoped I was just crazy.

"I wanted to pull you aside, to force you tell me what happened, but the word 'forced' made me realize it was the wrong thing to do and I needed to give you space. But I just knew. I could tell.

"It's like a light had gone out."

We both sat quietly for a minute, mourning a version of me that no longer existed.

"When you left for school...parting ways with you was... Elizabeth, it was the hardest thing I've ever done. Driving away, I didn't know if I was doing the right thing by not pushing. I wanted to talk to your Dad, but I knew that would take it out of your hands. I didn't know what to do.

"So I did the only two things I could do: First, constantly check on you, send you love, ask if you need anything, even as you pushed me away. I figured I'd just drive you nuts but at least you'd know I was there.

"And second: Stalk Rob and his pals around headquarters. I figured he might be stupid enough to brag about whatever did, or didn't, or almost happened. I doubted it'd be the truth, but I figured I'd learn <u>something</u> just by visiting and listening more often around your dad's office."

Her face went from sad to angry.

I tried to keep from reacting as she got more and more fired up with every word.

"I was right. He was stupid enough to talk about you on your father's property."

"What was he saying? What did you do?"

I could tell she didn't want to tell me what he said.

"Tell me."

"But, Elizabeth, you know what…it was muffled because I was outside, and the other guys were talking over him, and I didn't get every word."

"I want to know."

"The word-for-word doesn't matter. What matters is that he said enough to let me know that…"

"It matters to me, Gloria!" I shouted. And then, more quietly, "It matters to me."

"OK. Of course." And then, as if it gutted her to utter each and every word, she said, "He said, 'I gave it to Elizabeth the night of the party. She was so wasted she didn't even know that I was doing it until she woke up.'"

I sat there, looking straight ahead. I expected to feel angry. Sad. Hopeless. But I didn't feel any of that. I didn't feel anything.

Gloria was waiting for me to say something. And I knew it was time to tell her what happened, to share the burden. And I wanted to. But the words were beyond the strangle; they were just buried too deep to come out.

"Elizabeth, is that what happened? Did you wake up with him inside you?"

I nodded.

"Elizabeth." This time when she approached me, I let her. I collapsed into her arms and, finally, I cried. It felt like the first time in a year I was able to be the "Before" me again. A girl with hopes and dreams and a light that illuminated the innocence I still longed to have. Gloria held me and let all those months just bleed away with the loneliness, the guilt, the 3 a.m. wake-up calls from nightmarish echoes of *"I'm almost done – Just go back to sleep"* ricocheting around me as I imagined his gritted teeth as he thrust himself deeper inside me without a care.

After a while, she simply asked, "Is there anything else you want to share?"

"Not right now."

"OK. I understand. I'm here whenever you want to tell me more."

Gloria poured herself another shot of tequila and did it. Then, she turned back to me and grabbed my hand tight as she said, "I drove him out of town."

I almost started laughing, thinking she was making a joke. Then I looked in her eyes. She wasn't joking.

"I confronted him and said he had forty-eight hours to tell your dad that he's quitting and leaving town immediately to start a new job. If he didn't, or if he ever said your name again, even once, then I'd share with your Dad, and his family, and everyone he knows or ever tries to know, the recordings of him bragging about raping you."

"You got him on tape?!?"

"No, but he didn't know that. He quit that afternoon and left town a couple days later."

"<u>You're</u> the reason he did that?"

"Sure am."

"And you never told Dad?"

"I never told a soul, until now."

"Thank you," I whispered.

"I love you," she whispered back.

After a while of sitting quietly and sipping tea, she said, "Elizabeth, there are two things that I want to say. We won't linger on the first, unless you want to. For the second thing, I want to tell you, but once I do, I don't want to discuss it further so we can keep the focus on you and what you need in this moment."

"OK...?"

"The first is something I feel I <u>need</u> say: What Rob did is a crime. You could pursue legal action, if..."

I started shaking my head back-and-forth quickly and my breathing sped up.

"Of course...I get it...You don't want to. That's OK. Just know it's an option, someday, if you want it."

I nodded.

"The other thing I want to tell you is that I was date raped in my twenties, on a trip with some girlfriends."

"Gloria, I'm so sorry...I..."

"Thank you. But let's leave it there. Too many times, when a woman gets up the courage to tell someone they were raped, or abused, or molested, or...whatever...then, because there are just too damn many of us out there, oftentimes, the woman's big, brave moment is met with, 'Me too – I was, too,' which can be comforting after the fact, but in that exact moment, it can feel like the woman's one, singular story doesn't matter as much; like it's just one of many. And while, sadly, it <u>is</u> one of too many, it's still your trauma. It's specific. It deserves its moment. But just know, you are not alone."

"Thank you," was all I could manage.

"Elizabeth, was that night with Rob your first time?"

"No. Brendan and I were each other's firsts, and it was nice."

"Oh, thank God." Another tear streamed down her face.

I just nodded.

"Have you slept with anyone since then?"

"Not yet. It wasn't that hot of a freshman year." Neither of us laughed at my attempted joke.

"When you're ready, you'll know."

"Right now, I don't trust myself."

"Why not?"

"It's hard to put into words. It's like, I know it's not my fault. I don't think I deserved it. In fact, I know that I didn't. I know I said 'No' once I could..."

"I feel like there's a 'but' coming and I don't want to tell you how to feel, but...I hope there's no 'but' coming because that means you <u>do</u> feel guilty, on some level. And you should NOT, on <u>any</u> level."

"I know...*but*...I couldn't fight back, Gloria. I couldn't protect myself. I was so drunk that I had <u>zero</u> recollection of anything between puking and waking up with him inside me. And then I was useless. I couldn't fight back with any real force."

"Elizabeth...you shouldn't have to fight. You shouldn't have to wake up in that position, to..."

"I know. I know." But I didn't.

"Elizabeth, not being able to fight a 200-pound, full-grown male off of you while you were passed out...is...expected. What were you supposed to do? Drunk or sober? I'm trying not to tell you how to feel, but I hope you can feel, deep in your heart, that you have <u>zero</u> responsibility for what happened to you. You are brave, and beautiful, and smart, and aware, and...<u>not</u> responsible for the horror that happened to you."

We sat for a while. I had so much to say but, then again, I didn't. It just felt good knowing that I could talk, finally, if I wanted to. From then on. And to think she was here all along. For years. I was so busy missing a mother in my life, that I didn't open my eyes to the mentor who was in front of me the whole time.

"Have you told Ruth what happened?"

"No. I'm not ready."

"You've battled this so bravely on your own. And it was even braver to let me in. I just hope that you keep letting people in, telling people what happened. When you need to, for you. Not for anyone else."

"I know. And I will, but so far, I've adopted Alex's philosophy of: The bastard has already taken so much, I refuse to let him take any more from me. Not one day, or even one moment, letting it get me down, rehashing it and holding onto it. I won't give that night – or him – that power over my life."

"Oh, good. So you do talk to Alex about this?"

"Yeah. Wait, no."

"OK...?"

"I mean, she knows what happened to me. Well, not what exactly. But that <u>something</u> happened to me. I've never told her the story, or his name, or anything, but she knows... she knows something happened. But, that's how she is. She doesn't dwell. I know a lot of things have happened to her but she refuses to let them get the best of her. That's how I want to be."

"Well, you can be however you want to be. But there's a difference here if Alex freely mentions what happened to her and then has that philosophy, but...you haven't actually mentioned it yet to anyone. Really."

"I know, believe me, it's not easy to carry around these lies that..."

"Elizabeth, you're not 'lying' by not sharing what happened to you."

"OK. Fine. Then it hasn't been easy to keep this secret for so long..."

"I hate to cut you off again, but I have to. You're not lying or keeping secrets. The older you get, you'll start to decide to keep things more private than others. But you're not telling lies or hiding secrets. That sounds so sinister. And you're not."

"I guess, but…"

"Let's call what you're keeping an 'unspoken truth'. It's your truth. And you're keeping it to yourself. It's your story – it's your right – to do just that. And that takes the blame off yourself. It's such a small thing, but can you see the difference?"

I could. And that felt better. Lighter. I smiled.

"There's that smile," Gloria smiled back at me. "We can talk all night, but I'm starving. Should we call for pizza? Are you sleeping here? I hope so."

"I'd love pizza. I'd love to stay here. Can I take a quick shower and then borrow some PJs?"

"Yup. I'll put some in your…in the guest room for you."

I stood up slowly from the couch and looked at this woman who wasn't my mother but was the closest thing I'd had to it in a long, long time. She didn't ask for anything except love. In that moment I knew she'd do anything for me. I crossed the room and for the first time in my life held my arms out wide for her and gave her the biggest hug I shared all year.

Chapter Sixteen

Before that night with Gloria, the closest I got to telling anyone what happened to me was about a month into school when I went to a "Women Take Back The Night" march because my dorm floor was going together, and I hadn't made any friends yet, so I figured I'd push myself out of my comfort zone and join them.

By the time we all started walking downstairs, dozens and dozens of women joined us and I lost track of anyone on my floor. When we got outside, I could see that every other dorm bordering the quad was emptying onto it. There were so many women – There must've been hundreds of us.

The mood was somber. The volume nearly silent. Someone was handing out candles and another was following her, lighting them for people. And then a woman walked up to the podium and welcomed us by sharing that she was a Rape Survivor.

How did she do that? How did she stand there, so confidently, and announce that?

She said that one in four of us have been, or will be, raped.

"That's a lot of women. That's a lot of voices. Let's use them. Let's raise them!" she yelled into the microphone as the deafening silence erupted into women hollering.

And then, from different parts of the quad, a chant started – a few disparate groups at first, from different corners – until they all found their unison: "Women Unite – Take Back the Night," they yelled. And the group started to shuffle, one small step after another because that's as fast as you could walk with that many people moving as one unit.

I couldn't yell with them. I couldn't speak. I kept walking, alone, mouthing the words, tears streaming down my face. I felt alone, but supported. Shuffle step after shuffle step. Once we left campus and were on the street, we could pick up a little speed and, as I looked around, I realized I didn't recognize anyone. I wasn't scared, but I was done with being there. I didn't want to march alone. I didn't want to hear the sad stories when we all ended up back in the quad. I wanted to run. Literally. So I peeled off from the group.

But when I left the support of the group, my heart started racing as I tried to push the memories – and a panic attack – away. I found a tree to brace myself against while I tried to retain control of my breath.

Then I heard, "Hello, my name is Angela. I'm not a threat. I'm here to help, if you need me."

I froze.

"I'm going to approach you, unless you don't want me to," she said as she edged closer with a comforting smile. "I'm a student counselor. I travel with these marches to keep an eye out for people who might need to talk."

She now stood a few feet away from me. "Are you OK? Do you want to talk?"

"I don't know." I really didn't know how to answer. I wanted to talk, but I didn't know what to say, where to start. It's like the words were lodged in my throat, and if I let them out, they'd be too big to broker. For some reason, it felt better to bottle them up, even as they drowned me.

How could I explain my swirl of emotions? The guilt I felt about how drunk I was; about how I couldn't protect myself. I knew it wasn't my fault – I knew that in my core – but I didn't feel blameless. I was riddled with shame. And guilt. And outrage. And anger. How could I explain that? Where did I start?

"Did something happen to you or someone you love?"

I nodded.

And then we sat there, under a tree, just off the route where hundreds of women marched past, using their voices as loud as they could. And I found my voice – a version of it at least – and told Angela what happened with Rob after the barbeque. I told her all of it, but still couldn't say the word for what he did to me. I found all the words to give her the play-by-play, but couldn't say that one word to sum it all up. But it didn't matter, because Angela said it for me. "Elizabeth, you were raped." I was able to nod, and when I did, it felt like the person who died that night in Rob's cottage came back to life with a little gasp. Just a little one. But it was enough.

I wondered in the months that followed, and even now, if Angela thought of me as often as I thought of her after that night. Probably not.

Sometimes, I wished I had her phone number.

Sometimes, I wondered if she was an angel.

SUNDAY

Chapter Seventeen

I was up early and anxious the next day, wanting to get to Sacred Art before packing up and leaving for school. I had a rough night's sleep, tossing and turning as I tried to organize my thoughts on everything from gratitude for Gloria for being the reason Rob left, to absolute confusion that, regardless, she probably had been lying to me about Mom's letters for years. But maybe Dad convinced her to keep them from me? But did that justify it?

I couldn't stop thinking about how, right now, Gloria was my only sounding board. I went around and around in my head, wondering <u>why</u> I didn't want to call Alex or Ruth. Shouldn't I <u>want</u> to share these things with my best friends? I mean, I kind of told Alex. But I minimized it.

What would she say if I told her that I battle the memories daily?

What if I stopped mirroring her, "Life sucks, let's move on," mentality and really delved into it?

What if I told her that part of the reason I didn't want to live off-campus was because I'd be afraid to be alone when she's out? And I'd be afraid to cry out from nightmares when she was home? It wasn't an issue this summer, but Provincetown felt a lot safer than Boston; and it allowed me to live in the present more than the past.

I got up and headed to Gloria's room. The door was ajar so I said, "Knock, knock." She was reading in bed and patted the spot next to her, "Good morning, come sit. How'd you sleep?"

I jumped on the bed beside her. "Not great."

"You have a lot going on. That's understandable."

If she only knew just how much more I was battling.

"Anything in particular bothering you?"

I almost blurted out that I found the letters, but I didn't. Instead, I shared, "You know, I was thinking about my friends, and how I haven't told them yet. I don't know what that's about. Me? Or them?"

"Friendship can be tricky sometimes. Especially the ones that last years and years."

"It seems like your friends are everything to you. I mean, look what you did for Dad. Just coming here, to help us."

"Me coming here helped me, too."

How was I this old and never really asked Gloria more about her life?

"How did it help you?"

She paused. "Well, there's a reason my life coaching business is called Glory Days. The tagline is 'From Gloria's Daze to Glory Days.'"

I had never really thought about it.

"Why were you in a daze?"

She chuckled, "Good question." I could see her get lost in her memories for a moment.

"Too many gambles, with my heart and with my health. Too much waste, of my time and my talent. My treasure. But that's a story for another day. Maybe for another weekend."

"I'd like to hear it."

"I'll look forward to that someday."

"Me too."

I wanted to say more, to thank her, to tell her that I was sorry I never...I don't know...that I took her for granted, that I resisted her for so long, in the ways that mattered. But I didn't want to say all those things only to learn shortly that she had been betraying me this whole time.

As if she could read my mind, she said, "Relationships are long. There's room for so much to happen, between you and your friends. Your current friends. Old friends. New friends.

"Do you know why I've had that worn-out blanket on my couch year after year, no matter what else about the room changes?"

"Because it's so comfortable...?"

"No. I mean, it is. But..."

"Because everything else you own is either cream or beige, so you need all the color in that blanket?"

"Ha! True. I've never thought of that actually. But, no, not because of that.

"I keep it there, where I can see it every day, because it reminds me of my friends. All the different colors of threads, and all the different patterns they make, on their own or together, represent each and every one of them as individuals and different groups."

"Did you make it? I've never seen you knit before."

"No, a friend of mine, Rachel, made it for me, and gave it to me on my fiftieth birthday, on a Girls' Trip to Mexico. She said it was an 'Old Lady Blanket' for when I was old, sitting in my rocking chair. She said it would keep me warm and it'd be like she was with me, no matter where we both were. And in her birthday toast that night, she explained how it's so colorful because I've lived such a colorful life, and that all the threads are pieces of my life, including everyone around the table that night and then some.

"I went into that trip feeling pretty low in life, for a bunch of reasons. It was back during my daze…I just…wasn't myself. I had been beat down a few too many times and I was having trouble rallying. But I thank my Lucky Stars every day for that trip, because it brought me back to life. For the first time in months – years, really – I felt like myself again. I got back from that trip and found myself dancing in the car again. I went from isolating myself from people who loved me, to reconnecting, to remembering what it felt like to be alive and energized and…I started my business after that. I came back to myself after that. And then…

"Not six months later, Rachel died in an accident."

"Wait, she what?!?"

"Yeah…she died. Swimming in the ocean one day, like she did most days."

"Oh my God. Gloria." Again, I was struck by how little I'd listened – or asked – about Gloria's life. How had it been all about me for so long? "Wow…I'm so sorry. She was fifty?"

"Yeah. Barely fifty. But, you know, she lived so big, so on her own terms, and was so generous and…I have to believe that, on some cosmic level, she knew she'd only get fifty years. And boy did she make the most of them. Her example, in how she lived and how she died, snapped me up and out of the low place I was in."

I wondered what, or who, would snap me out of this place I was in. I wondered if Alex, or Ruth, or anyone, could. What was I waiting for to share with them? What was that about?

I wondered what the pattern would look like in my own Old Lady Blanket?

"Elizabeth, I thought a lot last night, too. I thought about what you said. About the nuances of it all. About how you know it's not your fault, but that you don't feel blameless. About you trying not dwell on it, or let him take another moment from you. I thought about it all, all night long.

"You astound me for your ability to process this, to try to make sense of it, to own it in your own, quiet, solitary way. I'll think about all you said for months to come. So, thank you. And I hope that you'll think about the nuance between not letting him take your power, and not dwelling on it, but at the same time, making it part of your story by talking about it. Being more open about it, so you can really process and heal from it. I know you're not ready just yet. But please promise me you'll stay open to opening up eventually."

"I promise," I whispered, because if I said it any louder, it would trigger tears, and even if they'd be tears of gratitude, I was all cried out. I needed to put my game face on if I was going to confront Dad before I left.

I stole a line from Alex and said, "Let's do this goodbye like pulling off a bandage – really quick – so I don't cry."

"OK, I get it. I love you. I'm here for you. I'm proud of you. I believe in you. You're a Survivor. You know that, right? Even if you can't say it yet, you know it, right?"

I nodded.

"As hard as this moment is, Elizabeth, I don't worry about you. I know you will thrive, in spite of this. You have already been asked to endure and transcend more than most. And I have complete faith that you will continue to conquer whatever challenges are put in front of you.

"I always told your Dad that he should've named you Pearl because you were blessed with grit <u>and</u> grace."

"Thank you."

"And, someday, you might consider sharing all this with him, Elizabeth. Even though he's tough, he's one of the most sensitive people I've ever met. And I know there's even a secret place where he still holds his love for your mother. A place that he keeps from us."

"The safe?"

"No. Well, sure, the safe – I don't know what's in there – but I meant his heart."

Chapter Eighteen

When I pulled into the driveway, Dad was waiting at the front door, smiling.

It felt like I was moving in slow motion as I turned off the ignition, gathered my things, and made my way towards him. It felt like crossing a muddy mile, yet, I arrived before I was ready.

As I approached, he said, "We have the whole day together. Finally. I've been looking forward to this since you left a year ago."

"We need to talk," is all I said as I went by him, dropped my keys in the bowl on the table inside the door, kicked my shoes off, and walked over to the couch where I curled up in a blanket and just waited. I wanted to be my own, tight little unit for this conversation.

Dad followed me in. "What's wrong, Honey?" he said as he came towards me.

"Don't, Dad," I snarled, and my scowl told him to keep his distance.

"What's wrong?"

"Dad, I found them."

"Found what?"

I just stared at him.

"Honey, you're scaring me. What's happening?"

"I found the letters."

"Wait, what?"

He came towards me.

"Don't!" I put my hand up. "Just. Don't."

We locked eyes. I fought my tears back. I wanted to be angry, not sad. Or disappointed. I <u>didn't</u> want to cry.

I ratcheted up my fury. "Do you have <u>anything</u> to say, or are you trying to figure out which lie to tell me next?"

Dad just stood there, only a few feet in front of me, but he might as well have been on Mars. "I...I don't know what to say...I..."

"You don't know what to <u>say</u>, Dad? How about 'I'm sorry' right off the fucking bat?"

"Honey...I...I was trying to protect you..."

"From who? Mom? What are you talking about, Dad?" My voice got louder and louder until I was shrieking.

"Honey, calm down."

"STOP CALLING ME THAT! AND STOP TELLING ME WHAT TO DO. Those days are OVER!"

"OK...OK. Of course. I understand."

"No, Dad. You <u>don't</u> understand. And you <u>don't</u> get to be the reasonable, wonderful man I thought you were. You don't get to be calm and calm me down. You blew that with me. Forever." And then something from deep down inside screamed its way out of me, "WHAT THE FUCK DID YOU DO Dad?"

"I was trying to protect you, Elizabeth."

"What does that even mean? Is there more to this story than I gathered from the letters? Is she some kind of a monster or something?"

"No, but...she wanted to leave, Elizabeth. She left. I was doing the best I could and I had my reasons for not sharing those letters with you."

"It wasn't your decision to make, Dad!"

"I know. I <u>don't</u> know. I..." He started walking towards me, but I put my arms up as a barrier again. "Don't you dare try to hug me right now."

He put his hands up and backed away. "OK, I understand."

He settled on the chair across the room.

"Does Gloria know?"

"No. She doesn't. I've almost told her a million times. Just like I've almost told you a million times."

"Then why didn't you?"

"I don't know. I...I just don't know. Maybe if Gloria had been here when the letters first arrived, then I would've asked her opinion. But by the time she got here, Mom had stopped writing."

"What do you mean she stopped writing? There was more than what's in the safe?"

He looked down.

"Dad, did she send more than those two letters?"

He looked up. "Yes."

My heart snapped in two like a cold twig when I thought of Mom, waiting for me to respond. Waiting for me to give her a signal that she should fight for me. What did she think? What did Dad say? She must've asked why I wasn't writing to her, or getting on the phone, if they spoke.

"What did you say to her?"

"What do you...when...?" he stuttered to stall.

"She must've asked, Dad! What did you tell her when I never wrote back?"

"That you were busy and..."

"Every time?

"Honey, there weren't that many times. She disappeared and left..."

"What. Did. You. TELL. Her?"

"That you didn't want to talk to her."

There it was. It felt like a punch to the gut.

"Is there no end to your lies? What else don't I know? Jesus Christ, Dad!"

Silence.

"It's not rhetorical, Dad. What else are you keeping from me? Give me a fucking answer."

"Watch your language, please."

"Fuck off."

Silence.

"Dad, where are the other letters?"

"I threw them away. I..."

"You did WHAT?!"

He kept his voice calm, almost like he was talking to a small child. "None of them ever had a return address. She never said where she was living. Honey, they weren't even really to you. They were all about her. They were angry, selfish letters to me with notes for you. Some of them didn't even make sense towards the end."

"I can't believe you're justifying this right now."

"Honey, beyond the letters, we spoke a handful of times. She always called from a new number. She never gave me a mobile number for her."

Silence.

"As much as it pains you, and as much of a shock as finding these letters must've been, it stands that she didn't want to be found. She didn't want us to be in her life, or she would've tried harder."

"She didn't want YOU to be in her life, Dad. YOU. She wanted me. She wrote to me. She asked for me. If you had only let me talk to her, let us decide...If you had..." I started sobbing as I thought of all the lost years...all the times my heart broke and re-broke when I thought she didn't think about me after she left. All the questions I had about why she left, and where she went.

"Elizabeth, think about after she left. You always said you HATED her. I figured she had done irreversible damage. At least for the time being. And, it's not like she showed up – actually showed up here for you."

I stayed silent and still. That's all I could manage.

"Elizabeth, I don't know if you remember, but you were CRUSHED when she left. We were broken, barely hanging on. And just because some sporadic letters and phone calls were made, I didn't trust her. I was protecting you. I knew she'd bail again."

"It wasn't your place to decide whether or not to give me the letters! To keep them from me for all these years, making me think that she left and <u>never</u> looked back. And making her think I was <u>choosing</u> to ignore her. It's so FUCKED UP, Dad. How can you not see that? How can you still say you were protecting me? How will I <u>ever</u> trust you again? Trust <u>anyone</u>?"

"Please don't say that. You can trust me. If I could go back, I'd..."

"What? Let me have a proper goodbye with my mother? Not keep the letters from me? Let me build a relationship with her, even if she didn't want one with YOU anymore?"

"That's not fair."

"Not fair!?!? YOU'RE going to lecture me about FAIR? That's rich, Dad – That's real..."

"SHE DIDN'T EVEN WANT YOU IN THE FIRST PLACE!"

I gasped.

And then it was silent. Dead, cold silence.

"Dad...what did you just say?"

"I'm sorry. I lost my temper. I shouldn't have said that."

"What do you mean?"

Silence.

"Dad, what do you mean?"

"Elizabeth…It was a long time ago. I know your mother loved you. Loves you."

"Dad…TELL ME WHAT YOU MEAN."

Silence.

"Dad, I'll get up right now and walk out if you don't explain yourself."

"When your mother got pregnant with you, she was supposed to show at an up-and-coming gallery in the Village. The dates of the show were your due date. She thought that, maybe…That, maybe it wasn't the best timing for a baby. She knew she had a dream that she wanted to pursue. A dream she had long before she dreamed of being a mother."

"So why didn't she get rid of me?"

Dad looked down and then up, straight in my eyes. "<u>We</u> agreed to have the baby. And your Mom got…" He teared up. "She got really excited about you. She wept with me many times, saying that she couldn't believe she ever considered not having you. She was excited about being a mother and she was convinced she could be both a mom and an artist. She committed to the art show and worked so hard to get ready for both of you.

"But she pushed it. She worked too hard. She ended up on bed rest for the final three months of her pregnancy, which slowed her progress for the show. And she had to back out of the show."

"And she blamed me."

"No! This is why I should NEVER have let that slip. She never once doubted wanting to be your mother."

"Until she left me."

Dad didn't say anything.

After a little while, Dad broke the silence. "If there had been any consistency to her attempts, then I would've facilitated you and her connecting. But, Honey, and it hurts me to say this because it will hurt you, she wasn't trying that hard. She left us."

Chapter Nineteen

I remember Dad yelling at Mom.

"Evangeline, you can't just GO AWAY for a month. You're a MOTHER for God's sake."

I was supposed to be asleep upstairs, but it was impossible to sleep when they yelled. I had forgotten just how often they fought before she left. I'd always thought of Mom's departure as so sudden, but I was starting to see it as anything but.

"Mike, doesn't it mean <u>anything</u> to you that I was <u>accepted</u> for this? Aren't you proud at all? Can't you support me in this?"

"It's unrealistic. It just doesn't make sense. When you applied, I thought you were just doing it to see if you could get in. I didn't really think you thought you could leave for a month."

"But why not? I <u>could</u> leave for a month. If I were an actress on location or..."

"But you're NOT, Eve. And you're not going to work to earn money. You want to go on a vacation and leave your child and…"

"I already told you that I have Elizabeth covered between Alice, the Owens, and the Millers down the street. Sure, you'll have to do a <u>little</u> more, but don't you want to do it for me, Mike?"

"It's just not a reliable plan."

"Why not? Because <u>you</u> didn't come up with it?"

"No, because…Well, yeah, actually. You can't just go ahead and plan a month of our lives, telling all these wackos that we barely know, all about our schedules and…What were you thinking?"

"Wackos? Mike, these are my friends. You know Alice is dear to me. You know I trust the Owens. I thought you liked them."

"I do, as your part-time bosses who understand your commitment as a wife and mother come first. But this is <u>not</u> that."

"Well for FUCK'S SAKE, Mike. I guess the next time you have to cruise into the city for a business meeting for nights at a time, I won't bend over backwards to make it all work for you. I won't encourage you to go, do good work, have some fun."

"It's your JOB, Evangeline. You are a stay-at-home mother, <u>not</u> an artist. You will never earn decent money as an artist, and certainly not the kind that will keep us living the lifestyle we've all grown accustomed to, including you, my little artist-at-heart-with-a-mega-bank-account because of MY WORK."

It was silent after that for a little while. Then I heard Dad say, "I'm sorry. Don't cry. I know that was low. I do believe in your work."

I didn't hear another word. I wondered what would happen. Would Mom go? I remember I didn't want her to, but I <u>did</u> want her to be happy, and I knew that art made her happy. I sat there and listened for what felt like hours, but was probably only a little while. However long it was, it was dead silent. I could <u>feel</u> the silence from a floor away. When I couldn't take it anymore, I pulled the blankets over my head, cocooned even tighter in my blankets, and tried to sleep.

Chapter Twenty

As I drove from Dad's house to Sacred Art, I stopped rehashing my conversation with him long enough to realize that I had forgotten to call Alex back. She had called a few times and her last message said, "I'm getting kind of worried about you. What could you be doing in Wellbury that's more fun than catching up with me? You better be having fun. Call me. Let me know."

I dialed her number, ready to tell her as much as she had time to hear about.

It was time. It was needed.

Her phone rang and rang. And rang. My nerves were in high-gear but I knew I needed to start to open up. To share. To process. To heal.

Finally, her voicemail picked up. I let out a deep breath. Phew. But at least I tried. For that moment, that was enough. When I heard the beep of her outgoing message, I just said,

"Hi, thanks for checking on me. No, I'm not doing any-thing in Wellbury that's more fun than being with you. But, boy-oh-boy, have I been on one hell of a rollercoaster since I got back. Highs and lows. Lots of unexpected twists. Call me when you have a little bit of time. Everything is good. But I want to fill you in on some things. OK? Love you. Bye."

I got out of the car and walked into the store.

Mr. Owens lit up from behind the counter when I walked in.

"Hull-ooo, dear!" he shouted in his sing-song way.

"Hi, Mr. Owens! It's good to see you."

"And you, too, dear. You too. You must be dying to know what I found out."

Relieved he was cutting right to the proverbial chase, I smiled in an encouraging way.

My heart was in my throat.

Just then, the door opened and the bell jangled and Mr. Owen's attention was diverted.

"Hold on one minute, dear," he said and turned to the incoming customer, singing his "Hull-ooo."

I wandered away from the register and, as I roamed, I wondered where Josh was. Maybe out back? Would I ask to see him if he didn't pop out before I was about to leave? I tried to stop my racing thoughts as I browsed the aisles and waited for Mr. Owens to tend to the customer. As I strolled, I was reminded of what an absolute adventure it felt like to be in there as a little girl. Mom used to say, "I hate having to bring you to work with me," but I remembered loving it. All those art supplies and colors and ideas dancing about. And seeing Mom in her element. I wouldn't have called it that back then. I would've just thought it was Mom being Mom. But now that I'm older, and I know how many sides of ourselves we have, and how few we share, I could see how much she was herself here. And in her studio. And with me.

I'm struck with a pang of longing so hardcore that I take a quick breath in. As I'm looking down, singing the ABCs to distract myself from crying, my gaze falls upon the blank notebooks that Mom used to give me to write in while she painted in her studio. I grabbed the last three there.

At the counter, the customer was paying as I walked back up. Once they left, Mr. Owens turned his full attention to me. He spotted the notebooks. "Your mother will love that you grabbed those. She always hoped you'd have art in your life, in some way."

"She did?"

"Oh, sure. She thought it was fundamental to life. I suppose all artists do." He took the notebooks from me, put them in a bag, and slid them back across the counter.

"These are on me, but please make sure you send me some notes on some of the pages."

"It's a deal."

Mr. Owens was smiling and I didn't want the moment to end. It was just me and him, in this special place. For us. For that moment. Cut off from the outside world, despite the floor-to-ceiling windows on Main Street.

"I was able to connect with Alice."

"You did?"

"I did! Well, kind of. I spoke with her dog walker. Alice is away for a bit, at one of those artist camps she loves. She was always telling me and Mrs. Owens that we should go, but who can do that, we tried to explain. Not people with businesses, like we had. Anyway, she is away at one now."

"Oh, OK." I tried to hide my disappointment.

"But don't despair. The good news is that it's only a couple weeks. Not one of the longer ones she's done. She'll be back in two weeks. We just missed her."

"Did you say, 'two weeks'?"

"Yes, is that terribly long?"

"No! It's better than I thought you were going to say."

"Oh, right-o! Delightful! I explained to the lovely lady watching her dog that it's important that Alice call me soon after her return. I didn't say anything else so it wouldn't get jumbled in translation. But I know she'll call me. She always does. And as soon as she does, I'll call you. It won't be long now. I just know it."

I was happy he was optimistic and trying not to feel defeated.

Two weeks.

I tried to tell myself that I'd waited nearly two decades, so what's another two weeks?

"Excellent, Mr. Owens. Thank you."

He walked around the counter and wrapped me in a warm embrace. "Please keep in touch, Elizabeth. And please do well in school. And follow your dreams. I do hope that you and Evangeline are reunited soon." He paused, as if to ponder whether or not to say what he said next. "You know, I was always sorry that it didn't work out between your parents. There was a lot of love there. I hope you don't mind me saying, but I was thinking about it last night, and I think it was just the classic case of your mom always figuring he wouldn't change, and your dad always figuring she would."

"Thank you, Mr. Owens. I do appreciate that." I grabbed my notebooks and walked towards the door. I was so sidetracked by his insights about Mom and Dad that I almost – almost – left without asking. And then, once I remembered, I almost didn't turn around because I didn't want to ask Mr. Owens for any more favors, but then I thought, *Fuck it*, and turned around.

"One more thing, Mr. O."

"Anything, dear girl."

"What about Josh? Isn't today his last day?"

"Thank Heavens you asked! He would've never forgiven me if I had forgotten. He left about an hour ago. He asked me to give you this."

He rummaged around in his drawer again and pulled out another notebook, larger than the ones I had grabbed earlier. My name was written in the coolest script on the brown paper cover, like graffiti art. It was all I could do not open it right away, but I just took it and said, "Oh, great! Thanks!" and then I beelined it out of there.

When I was a few stores away, I stopped to read it.

On the first page he wrote, *I can't wait to see what you write. You can use these pages to jot down some ideas.* And then he gave his email address. The rest of the pages were blank.

I was already thinking of ways I'd fill them with plans and checklists and bits of info I found as I looked for Mom. I couldn't imagine ever actually sending something for Josh to read, but the idea of it sparked in my chest. For the first time in a long time, I felt joy. Simple, straightforward joy.

As I got ready to cross the street, I looked up, and, coming towards me, were Brendan and Abby. Her arm was looped through his elbow, and she was so sure that he'd guide her, that she was looking down and talking a mile-a-minute. He was looking up, straight at me with a sheepish expression. When we passed right by each other, he mouthed, "I'm sorry."

I just smiled.

It was all good.

At least, it would be.

I was settling myself in the car, programming the GPS and planning my road trip playlist when I saw that Dad called while I was in the store. His message begged me to come to talk about something that was time-sensitive, and that he wanted to say goodbye one more time. I sat there debating what to do. Most of me wanted to drive back to Boston and leave Dad far behind until I could process the last few days. But part of me was curious about what was time-sensitive, and, yes, a part of me even wanted to see him again.

I started driving.

When I pulled into the driveway, he was waiting at the door.

"I'm so glad you came, Honey."

"I'm busy, Dad. Let's not make a big production out of whatever you're about to say," I said as I breezed by him and into the kitchen. "What's up, Dad? I really should get going."

"I know. Look, I can't stop thinking about this. I can't stop thinking of ways to make it right. And, I know I can't.

Not really. And I'm sorry for that. I'm sorrier than you'll ever know, Elizabeth.

"And I know we have so much more to talk about. And so much work ahead of us. And I hope that you want to do both the talking and the work. I hope. Though I know you might not. And I'm prepared for that. Though I'd hate it."

"Dad…"

"Please, let me finish.

"I know that I can't change what I did. If I could, I would. But I can't. And I don't know how you and I move forward from here. But I do know I can give you some options from here."

"Dad…"

"Wait, Elizabeth. Let me finish. I called the school and explained that we have an unexpected family emergency."

"What? Why?"

"Elizabeth, I want to give you two options and I'll fully support either one, financially and otherwise. You can go back to school as planned, and I'll support you finding Mom from there, however you can. Or, I'll support you deferring for a semester so you can find her with zero distractions."

I didn't have any words, so I just started to cry.

"If you defer, you can stay with me, or Gloria, of course, or…"

"Dad, STOP! Just stop. You don't get it, do you? You can't fix this now. You denied me the chance to know my mother. You stole years and years from me. From her. I barely recognize the girl I was when she was still here; a girl who made art and danced and giggled. When's the last time you heard me laugh, Dad, let alone giggle?"

"Honey, I..." he stepped towards me.

"No." I put my hand up. "NO." I shook with emotion. "I mean, would she even know me if she saw me?"

We looked each other in the eye for a moment, both fighting back tears.

"I have to go."

"Wait, Honey, let me finish..."

"WHAT, Dad?! Just spit it out!"

"You could start to look for Mom immediately with this." He pulled a manila envelope from behind his back and handed it to me. "It's the last known address for her. I did try to find her a while back and I almost did, but then I thought, *What will that do? She wanted to leave. What would I do? Insist she come back?* So I stopped looking. But that is where I would've gone next. It was only eight years ago."

I stared at the document in front of me. It was from a private investigator. It said Mom was living in Baja California, Mexico. What could she be doing there? I just sat there, my head spinning.

"Elizabeth, I'd bet my life that she's still in that area. You could go there."

I didn't know what to say.

Dad plowed on. "I'd love to say, 'Take your time' and 'Think it over as long as you need to' but I can't because, you can't. The school needs an answer soon."

"I need to think."

"Of course. It's a lot to think about. There's something to be said for you heading back to school, staying focused on that. Let's make a pros and cons list and…"

"Dad, NO. Please, just stop. I've got it from here."

"But you'll need money if you…"

"Dad, I have money. I worked hard this summer. I saved. I'm doing this on my own."

"But…"

"Dad. Enough. Just…enough."

"Wait, just one more thing – I'll be right back," he said and I sighed. He zipped into his office for a second and returned with a stack of postcards.

"These are yours. Thirty of them. From Mom. She did write every day that she was gone at that camp."

"I thought you said you got rid of all her letters?"

"I did throw away the letters that came after she left the art camp. They were angry letters. They were really to me with mentions to you, like, 'Tell Elizabeth that I love her.'

"But these were from her in those first thirty days she was away. I thought I had them tucked away somewhere in storage, but I didn't want to promise them and not deliver when you confronted me yesterday. But I found them. And they're yours. They're beautiful. And they're all true, Elizabeth. Each and every one of them."

"What are they...what did she...?" I start flipping through them, but couldn't even process what I was looking at.

"Each one has one message on it; one thing she loves about you. They're simple. And Sweet. And I just couldn't throw them away. Maybe, on some level, I knew we'd get here someday."

He was looking at me like he was waiting for something. I knew he wanted forgiveness or, at the very least, a "thank you" for the postcards. I couldn't muster either.

"I have to go."

Dad looked the closest to crumbling that I'd ever seen when he realized that our conversation was over, that I was leaving. I gave a small wave from where I was standing.

There was a man I used to know who bounced me on his knee. A man who was bronzed and strong from working in the sun, yet, soft enough to sing me "Stairway to Heaven" like a lullaby because it was the only song he could ever remember all the words to without it playing in the background. This man would hug me, and kiss me, and stay up sitting in a chair in my room until I fell asleep when I was scared. This man showed me love. He showed me protection. And I basked in it; yet I was blinded by it. Because now I saw what I couldn't see before.

It wasn't me who was scared. It was him. He'd always been scared. Scared we'd have no money. Scared of Mom being too carefree with me. Scared of truly letting someone live without his big arms protecting them.

I saw that day the man he'd always been: The one trying to keep me safe and protect me from everything. From pain, from lies, and, by extension, from real love.

I looked at him one last time. His face looked older, his tan paler, his eyes duller. I resisted the urge to tell him it was all OK. Because it wasn't.

I turned towards the door and walked out.

The day was turning to night as I pulled out of the driveway and silently prayed for a sign, for something to guide me from here.

As I rolled out of Wellbury and onto the highway, I turned on the radio.

Three Little Birds poured out of the speakers.
Rise up this mornin'
Smile with the risin' sun

Three little birds

Pitched by my doorstep

Singin' sweet songs

Of melodies pure and true

Sayin', "This is my message to you, whoo-hoo...

And, just like that, I knew what I needed to do.

-The End-

Resources

If you or someone you love has been sexually assaulted and you need immediate support, you can call the National Sexual Assault Hotline at 1-800-656-HOPE (4673) or visit online.rainn.org

If you are a Survivor of sexual assault and are searching for ways to restore yourself, consider The Joyful Heart Foundation (www.joyfulheartfoundation.org) as a resource for healing.

About The Author

Courtney K. Hurst has chased enough dreams that, if her life were an amusement park, she'd have a "Grand Reopening" every decade with a new theme. She has succeeded and failed - personally and professionally - enough to learn that the biggest gifts you can give yourself are appreciation and forgiveness, whether you're winning or losing. Courtney hopes her books reveal how character is defined through the choices we make in the midst of change. Look for her at college campuses across the country talking about her own rollercoaster of a life, and the tools she uses to control her own tracks.

Acknowledgements

I used to read Acknowledgements and hope that, someday, I too would find an editor who I "couldn't have done it without" and who "the book is better because of." After a couple of failed attempts, my sister introduced me to Mick Thyer and, finally, I found my editor. Mick, I couldn't have done it without you and this book is better because of you. To Manuela Gomez Rhine, thank you for tightening it up. And to Chrissy Stalions, your cover will make it sell. Thank you for sharing your talents with me.

Long before I was ready to hand it over to those three, some friends doubled as "Beta Readers" and helped me get closer to what Elizabeth's journey needed to be: Adi, Amber, Anne, Ashley, Christina, Dawn, Eliza, Emily B., Gretch, Halc, Jan, Jeanette, Julie, Katie, Liv, Maddie, Mariana, Maya, Melanie, Mom, Nancy, Sabine, and Sarah, you read some pretty brutal, early drafts and you kept me accountable, but encouraged. Thank you for both. To my interns: Sailor and

Farrah. Thanks for keeping me current with your youth and your research. To Dawn and Jan, my unofficial publishing team, thank you for the many ways you helped get me here.

Now comes the challenging part: Trying to acknowledge every thread from my own "Old Lady Blanket." To go person by person, year by year would be impossible. There are just too many of you; and for that, I am blessed. It's my goal to write enough books to acknowledge each and every one of you; but here's a start:

Mom, you're the batting of the blanket. You're the base. You're the warmth. Gretch and Halc, without you two zigging and zagging across my entire blanket, it wouldn't hold together. Without you, I come apart. Jack, Sailor, Wade, and F.J., you're my corners; it starts and ends with you. Johnny, thanks for being a solid stripe for as long as I can remember. Emanuel, your thread showed up right on time. And thank you, Aunt Halcyone and Aunt Kathie, for the holes you helped me patch along the way. Dad, your colors are constant, even though you're gone.

Thanks to all my friends from my cherished childhood days in Provincetown, and especially to Adi, Katie, and Sherry for making sure there's orange and black in every section of my blanket, no matter what else changes.

Thank you to the old threads who still feel new, like Chad and Myya; and new threads that already feel old, like

David and Bill. To youthful "summer friends" who turned lifelong, like Erika and Sarah. To The Surf Club Crews, from all the years, and, of course, to the ones who kept showing up, decade after decade, long after we had slung our last fish & chips: Amber, Katie, and Melanie.

To Cheryl, Duder, and Kate. It's hard not to think of you – and feel eternally grateful for you – when writing about college life. And in so many ways, my blanket wouldn't have been so wonderfully woven without Cathy's friendship, and the golden threads of the Metis Years. (Shout out to The OG Metis Team.)

Finally, to the forever friends who rallied when I needed them most, to remind me just how comforting my blanket can be if I let it: Dawn, Jan, Michelle, Gretchün, Halcyone, Elisa, Katie, Melanie, and Rachel. Thank you.

# # #